Wasteland and Other Stories

Robert Perron

Published by And Then Press, 2024.

This is a work of fiction. Similarities to real people, places, or events are entirely coincidental.

WASTELAND AND OTHER STORIES

First edition. December 4, 2024.

Copyright © 2024 Robert Perron.

ISBN: 979-8991833813

Written by Robert Perron.

Table of Contents

Introduction	1
Azaleas	2
A Joke for Chong	17
Class of '65	19
Men at War	23
Low Speed Jet	30
Government Issue	35
Rearguard	50
Wasteland	58
What About India?	69
There You Go	85
Hippasus of Metapontum	95
Negative Entropy	102
Mind Over Matter	105
The Pugilist	118
Sunrise Cliff	125
Ole Ned	127
Exodus	143
Cover and Publication Credits	157

In memory of Lore Segal

Introduction

This collection of previously published stories highlights the resilience of the human spirit when faced with threats to well-being and survival.

The first seven stories focus on soldiers and their experiences. In "Azaleas," a veteran in war-torn Korea grapples with his future. "A Joke for Chong" offers a brief snapshot of life on the front lines. "Class of '65" reflects on the aftermath of a fatal firefight. Both "Men at War" and "Low Speed Jet" delve into life on the home front during the Vietnam War. In "Government Issue," military justice proves as destructive as combat. "Rearguard," a home front story set during the Iraq War, rounds out the soldier tales.

"Wasteland," the collection's title story, begins in reality and slips into a dreamlike state, as the protagonist grasps not so much for physical survival as for a meaningful existence.

The next seven stories explore contemporary life, with a nod to ancient Greece. "What About India?" and "There You Go" examine how both white- and blue-collar workers rely on employment not only for income but for their sense of self-worth. "Hippasus of Metapontum" warns of the dangers of introducing revolutionary ideas into society. In "Negative Entropy," a flash fiction piece, new ideas collide with old, destructive behaviors. "Mind over Matter" follows a protagonist grappling with the consequences of her actions in difficult circumstances. Similarly, in "The Pugilist," the main character drifts between reality and a self-created illusion. "Sunrise Cliff," a flash, rekindles—or perhaps doesn't—a romance.

The final two stories, "Ole Ned" and "Exodus," set in the near future, imagine Canada's immigration challenges as its southern neighbors flee increasingly uninhabitable environments.

Azaleas

Downhill a few kilometers, at the edge of the village, Sang-min found a drinking house. Outside leaned bicycles piled high with thatched baskets. Inside men sat on mats around low tables, the room warm, twisting with tobacco smoke. Heads turned to take stock of the young stranger: worn combat boots, faded field jacket, military knapsack.

A familiar voice said, "So I guess you're discharged."

Sang-min smiled. He had stopped to inquire but here sat Jae-wook, the object of his inquiry. Jae-wook, businessman of necessity, poet and philosopher at heart, or so he proclaimed. At the start of the war, Sang-min had been drafted to the infantry (despite two years of university), wounded by shell fire, and transferred to a supply depot run by Jae-wook, older, a civilian. The two men shared talk and books. They reviewed their woes, how the slaughter of his platoon pounded Sang-min's ears as medics evacuated him, how Jae-wook watched his father and brother blindfolded and shot on charges of collaboration. Sang-min would recite: "'If man is born to live, / what should I worry? / Man lives till he dies.'" Jae-wook's eyes and lips would glisten: "Ah, the poetry of Kim So-wol."

Soju was poured and wine bowls lifted.

"My young friend, what are you doing up here?"

"You invited me."

"Hah. But I never thought you'd take me up on it, come to such a godforsaken place."

"There's no work in Seoul. And Pusan?" Sang-min's family had fled to the bottom of Korea ahead of the first invasion and stayed. But Sang-min, the lesser son, rebellious, never getting on with his father, jaded by the ways of war, had no desire to join them. He wanted to make his own life.

"So I thought I'd walk north and look up my old counselor."

"Well I'm glad you're here." Jae-wook tapped the side of his head. "I've had an idea brewing."

Sang-min laughed. Always a plan.

Jae-wook leaned forward. "But it may take some time. There are contingencies beyond my control."

Sang-min drank from his wine bowl then motioned south in the direction of the back road he had descended. He described a small farm on a sharp corner in the hills with a woman and two foreign-looking children. "They seem to be alone. Do you think she'd take on help?"

An old man coughed and spit on the floor. He wore the white flowing robe, white baggy pants, and high black hat of a provincial elder. His goatee fluttered wispy white and he smoked a long, bamboo-stemmed pipe.

Jae-wook said, "Let's take a walk."

Outside, shops bent into the dust of the main road. Traffic moved by foot, bicycle, and ox cart. Bouncing mini-buses converged at a plaza of packed dirt in the village center. Military vehicles abounded, mostly American—jeeps and diesel-spewing trucks. On the far side of town, Sang-min made out the middle expanse of the Imjin River and its far bank where the no-man's land between the two Koreas began.

Jae-wook produced cigarettes and a narrative. The old man inside headed the Hwang family and controlled what wealth remained along this section of the river. The war had cost him both sons. His three daughters were married off, his wife dead. A mess for the future of the family, Jae-wook explained, with nephews and sons-in-law vying for power as old Hwang, indifferent, spent his time in drinking houses and brothels.

Jae-wook raised a finger. "But where there's a mess, there's opportunity." He had a cousin, daughter to his mother's sister, close in age to Sang-min, named Hyo-chu. Jae-wook suggested to Hyo-chu a match with old Hwang, was sure he could pull it off, that Hwang would not be able to resist a last conquest, a young bride of allure and elegance. Hyo-chu reacted with red-faced anger not about to waste her life on an old man. But that's the point, Jae-wook told her, he was old. "I'm guessing you pulled it off," said Sang-min. Indeed. Hwang slobbered in anticipation of the wedding night. The nephews and daughters expressed dismay but had no sway over the old man. As for Hyo-chu, she came to appreciate the folly of romance over security. After the wedding night and a few more nights, Hwang returned to the brothels. While he drank and fornicated, Hyo-chu secured leadership of the household, by nature gracious, not flouting her beauty. The daughters now adored her. Even the nephews had mellowed.

Jae-wook and Sang-min stripped their cigarettes military style, extinguishing flame with thumb and forefinger, tearing the paper, letting the tobacco flutter to the ground. Sang-min enjoyed Jae-wook's story-telling, the subtle changes of tone and facial expression, the sweeping gestures and intimations of confidence, but grew anxious as the talk drifted from his immediate concerns of food and shelter. He asked again about the woman in the hills with the small farm.

"She's Eun-mi," said Jae-wook. "Her family stayed put ahead of the first invasion. Big mistake. The northerners ripped them from their land. Eun-mi ended up in Dongducheon as a prostitute." Jae-wook paused. "But a savvy one."

"How so?"

"She came back with enough money to reclaim the farm. Although. Why bring those bastards? One looks half Chinese, the other American. Maybe not so savvy."

"What of her family?"

"Dead. Or taken north. Who knows? So she has title to the land, even as a woman. Hmm. Why not? Go see if she needs help while I sort things out here. Let me know if it doesn't work out."

• • • •

SANG-MIN RETRACED HIS steps on the primitive back road, steep and barren but for copses of leafless saplings, and arrived at the sharp corner above the small farm, where level ground formed a rough square a hundred meters to the side, sufficient for house, outbuilding, two small rice paddies, and a vegetable plot. Sang-min saw no oxen or pigs, but hens pecked the ground with alacrity, one strutting and squawking like a rooster. The narrow house had four raised rooms in tandem and a sunken kitchen whose stove pipe ran under their floors. A slim portico, no more than a shelf, fronted the house, with sliding doors giving entrance to the bantam rooms. A thatched roof extended over the portico.

Sang-min squatted and observed, not to spy, but to gather wit and nerve. A boy, close to four, with pronounced eye folds, on occasion glared at him. A round-eyed girl, two or three, waved. The woman, Eun-mi, ignored him. Her age seemed mid-twenties like his. They might have been siblings, both short with oval faces, flared nostrils, and wide mouths.

Sang-min squeezed the flame from his cigarette and sprinkled the remaining tobacco on the ground. He dropped from the road and approached Eun-mi who was striking the early spring earth with a hoe.

"It looks like you have a lot to do, what with the planting season upon us."

Eun-mi continued striking the ground. Sang-min saw that the round-eyed girl stood next to him and bent over extending his right forefinger.

"What's your name, little one?"

The child wrapped her hand around Sang-min's finger. "Hana."

"Hana, a beautiful name. My favorite."

Eun-mi stopped swinging the hoe and turned to Sang-min. "I see you're a great charmer."

"Look," he said, "I need employment. You need help."

Sang-min stood arms at side as Eun-mi made several more swipes at the earth before responding. "First, I can't pay much more than room and food."

Sang-min remained silent.

"Second. How do I know you're not a freeloader, or worse? Okay, we'll try it, but on probation."

• • • •

A WEEK LATER, SANG-min stood across the road by a stream, the water source for the farm. For washing, Eun-mi brought over clothes, soaking and pounding them on rocks. For other use, the water needed to be carried. Sang-min sank two buckets and pulled them out full. He ran a bamboo carrying pole under the handles, hefted, and balanced the buckets on his right shoulder. Crossing the road with the slopping water, he shook his head. Soon the paddies and field would require many such buckets.

Eun-mi looked up from the kitchen. "I have good news. Your behavior being exemplary, your probation is lifted." That evening Sang-min sat for the first time on the floor of the first room with Eun-mi and her children, Kyung-wan, the wary master, and Hana, as yet ebullient, holding bowls to their mouths, pushing in rice, kimchi, and boiled eggs.

"Is your room okay?" said Eun-mi.

"A bit cold at night."

"Yes, too far from the kitchen. Move next to us, to the second room."

Next day Sang-min dragged from the outbuilding a back carrier and addressed Kyung-wan who followed his movements. "Hey, little warrior. Do you want to help me today? Ask your mom if you can go into the hills." Sang-min hoisted the wooden frame to his back, crossed the road with Kyung-wan, and climbed for half an hour, until the farm appeared toy-like. "A little higher. On the top of this hill I'm sure we'll find many dead branches."

Sometimes the boy helped and sometimes he grew restless or tired. If restless, he ran across the hilltop with a stick fighting an imaginary foe. If tired, he lay on his back with arms askew. The warmer days made lying on the ground in the sun a comfort. Sang-min worked a steady pace, gathering thin, dead branches broken by winter's harshness. He cut or snapped them into meter lengths and laid them on the arms of the back carrier until they rose to its height.

. . . .

ONE MORNING, EUN-MI placed in Sang-min's hand a crumpled thousand-hwan note. They needed seeds and seedlings for planting as well as rice and vegetables to hold them over. Some dried fish if there was enough money.

"Cigarettes for yourself."

"Maybe some meat," said Sang-min.

"Too costly. We have kimchi and eggs."

In response, Sang-min addressed a delicate matter. The hen that strutted like a rooster was not laying eggs. She seemed to have the status of pet but these days pets were luxuries. And yes she would be a bit tough, but sufficient boiling would take take care of that.

Eun-mi interrupted. "You want to kill Hye-su?"

Sang-min closed his mouth, retreated to the second room, retrieved his knapsack, and set off for the village. He stopped at the drinking house and found old Hwang but not Jae-wook. Hwang's face was gaunt and his eyes red; he coughed and spit. Several men called out hello.

Sang-min found a grocery where he obtained everything, even dried fish. As the transaction concluded, Jae-wook appeared.

"It's about time you came down, Sang-min. We need to talk."

The two men ambled to the edge of town, arms behind their backs, chatting and nodding, down a path to the bank of the river. They peered across at American GIs in combat gear. They ambled back.

The Hwang family again. Jae-wook reviewed its current state, no sons, contentious nephews, sons-in-law who wanted a share of the wealth, Hyo-chu more and more the backbone of the household. Sang-min nodded, yes, he understood, had heard it before. Jae-wook previewed the state of the family once Hwang died. As his widow, Hyo-chu would be secure, in fact, rise to a position of semi-dominance. But Hyo-chu and the Hwang family would find the lack of a central male figure difficult. A marriage would be desirable but not a traditional one requiring Hyo-chu to leave the Hwang household with a dowry.

"Why are you telling me all this?" said Sang-min.

The men had stopped walking and were looking into each others' faces. Jae-wook laughed.

"Sang-min, we're looking for an upside-down marriage. Where the husband becomes part of the wife's household. We need a young man of small means but good ancestry, hard-working, amiable. It would help if he were handsome and literate, had some university. Knew some poetry."

Sang-min felt his face flush but regained composure and decided to join his friend's game. With flourishes of hand and voice, he told Jae-wook of a dream. Of the one dream that came every night to his cramped room on the impoverished farm. To some day take the hand of beautiful Hyo-chu and assume the role of patriarch of the mighty Hwang dynasty.

"I'm glad you're in good humor about this," said Jae-wook.

• • • •

UPON RETURN, SANG-MIN found Eun-mi in the kitchen. On the stove churned the stock pot letting off steam and a fragrance of knobby meat. A glance inside revealed Hye-su bereft of feathers and entrails. Eun-mi said, "I thought about it and you're right. That old hen was not pulling her weight."

At evening meal, Eun-mi asked about Sang-min's friend, the poet and philosopher Jae-wook, what plots was he hatching these days? How he had a toehold in the great Hwang family having arranged a match between its head and his cousin Hyo-chu. Had Sang-min heard the story?

With chopsticks halfway to her mouth, Hana said, "Mama, where did Hye-su go?" Kyung-wan chortled. Eun-mi raised a brow and bore its eye into Kyung-wan until he withdrew his smirk.

"Hye-su," Eun-mi said after a few seconds of thought, "has gone to the village to live with the great Hwang family."

Following supper, Sang-min crossed the road to the stream, removed his clothes, and washed everywhere despite the cold. The army had taught him hygiene. He could hear his squad leader exhorting him to cleanse all body parts including the covert. Sang-min thought back to the day he was wounded by mortar shrapnel and placed on a stretcher as Chinese bugles blared their advance. His squad leader squatted next to him and said, "Good luck, Sang-min. Maybe we'll get together in Seoul in better times." Two years later, discharged in Seoul, Sang-min found the residence of his former squad leader. His mother said he was still missing in action. Sang-min wanted to stay a while but the family didn't have enough to feed itself. That's when he decided to walk north and look up Jae-wook.

Sang-min recrossed the road and sat in the middle of the second room as the last daylight filtered through the small rear window. In front, the door slid open and Eun-mi entered carrying mat and blanket. She had decided to give over the first room to the children.

"The other rooms are cold. Do you mind if we sleep together?" Sang-min watched as Eun-mi squared her mat against his. He could smell the vigor of her body—she had given herself a good scrubbing too.

"This can't be permanent," said Sang-min.

"Nothing is permanent."

Several nights later they lay under blankets side by side, bare shoulder to bare shoulder.

"The children like you," said Eun-mi.

Sang-min was silent.

Eun-mi said, "Go ahead, say what you're thinking."

"I just wonder why you didn't give them over to one of the orphanages supported by the Americans?"

"Ha! You think I'm mushy-headed, don't you?"

"A bit. The children are a burden."

"They're not a burden. They're easy to care for. A bowl of rice, a pat on the head, a pat on the behind. As they grow, they'll help me on the farm. In my old age, they'll take care of me."

"So. You have it all worked out. And here I thought you were mushy-headed."

"Far from it." Eun-mi rolled toward Sang-min. She put a hand on his chest and her head on his shoulder. "I'm a practical woman."

• • • •

SANG-MIN PLANTED RADISHES, leeks and turnips, cabbages and sweet potatoes, cucumbers and beans. Rice seedlings filled the paddies. Soon Eun-mi made summer kimchi, salty and sour with pungency to bring a tear. Sang-min sold Eun-mi's kimchi at market. He sold eggs and bought chicks.

The hot months of summer passed.

Following the rainy season, the rice, cabbages, and turnips moved to maturity. Sang-min and Eun-mi spent their days bent over in the field and paddies. They stored cabbages and turnips for winter kimchi, keeping enough vegetables to cook fresh. The green rice stalks they cut by hand standing past their calves in the water of the paddies; by hand, they threshed and dried the stalks.

No news from the village.

One night during rainy season, Sang-min and Eun-mi had joined in intimacy and afterward lay talking as monsoon waters pummeled the roof.

"I must tell you something," said Sang-min. "Jae-wook thinks he can make a match between me and Hyo-chu when Hwang is gone."

Eun-mi said, "That's Jae-wook, forever looking to the main chance."

Sang-min sat up and scooted to the door. He slid it open, lit a cigarette, and, sitting cross-legged, blew blue smoke toward the sheets of water. Eun-mi came up behind and laid an arm over his shoulder. A surge of fondness enveloped Sang-min for this wartime prostitute.

"A dilemma," he said.

"No, it's not complicated at all." Eun-mi kissed the back of Sang-min's neck. "You'd be a fool to pass up such good fortune."

• • • •

BEFORE THE TIME TO start making winter kimchi, Jae-wook appeared on the path above the farm. He dropped from the road to where Sang-min and Eun-mi had unbent themselves in the field.

"Old Hwang has died."

Jae-wook wanted Sang-min to accompany him for a change of clothes then to pay respects. Sang-min countered that his attendance would be inappropriate.

"To the contrary, it's imperative."

Sang-min turned to Eun-mi, but she was gone, her hoe upon the ground.

The Hwang compound lacked the size and elegance of many Sang-min had seen in his travels, but north of Seoul appeared as Shangri-La. The rooms formed three sides of a large square with kitchens at both ends and a gated wall to the front, the courtyard clean and well packed, the covered portico that ran in front of the rooms wide.

"The Hwang family enjoys a first-rate homestead don't you think?" said Jae-wook. "They work all those paddies out back and have their hands in half the shops in town. See those two men in western suits?" Jae-wook pointed to two men in the middle of the courtyard smoking cigarettes.

"Nephews. One owns a grocery and is always traveling to Seoul. The other is in the local government."

Jae-wook guided Sang-min across the compound to a large room with many sliding doors. They sat on the portico to remove shoes. Jae-wook placed hwan notes in Sang-min's hand. "So you can make an offering."

They stood and Jae-wook opened a door. He put a hand in the small of Sang-min's back and his mouth close to Sang-min's ear. "You must be your most charming."

Jae-wook and Sang-min went first to the closed coffin where they made bows and offerings. After a time, they turned to where on the floor in mourning dress of white hemp sat the three daughters from the first wife, nieces, nephews, sons-in-law, and Hwang's widow, pulled back hair accentuating the delicacy of her face.

Hyo-chu stood and bowed. They sat, Sang-min facing Hyo-chu at two meters with Jae-wook between them back a little. Rice cakes, fresh autumn kimchi, and meat from a young dog appeared, along with tea. Hyo-chu thanked Sang-min for his presence. Sang-min extended condolences. There was talk of the weather, affairs of the village. Hyo-chu spoke in a low voice of moderate pitch.

"My cousin tells me you recite poetry."

Sang-min felt his face warming.

Jae-wook said, "Don't be bashful now. Give us some lines from Kim So-wol."

"'Azaleas' is my favorite," said Hyo-chu.

Sang-min put aside bowl and chopsticks. He knew the poem, everyone knew it. Jae-wook nodded. The words to the first verse came. "When you leave, / weary of me, / without a word I shall gently let you go." Sang-min evoked the second verse. "From Mount Yak / in Yongbyon / I shall gather armfuls of azaleas / and scatter them on your way."

"So melancholy," said Hyo-chu. "So lovely."

Jae-wook laughed. "Okay, Sang-min, we'll let you off the hook for now."

Afterward, in the courtyard, Sang-min and Jae-wook lit cigarettes.

"That went very well," said Jae-wook. "They're taken with you."

"Yes," said Sang-min, peering into the mountains.

Jae-wook followed his gaze. "Sang-min, there's nothing up there. Your future is here."

The nephew who owned a grocery and wore a western suit approached, bowed to Sang-min, and said, "Welcome, uncle."

Jae-wook said, "Please, no bad jokes at this time."

The grocer laughed addressing himself to Sang-min. "When Hyo-chu came here as Hwang's wife, I called her aunt even though she was ten years younger. Now I'll be calling you uncle. But you strike me as a man we can rally around. I'll be happy to show you the ropes."

When they were alone again, Jae-wook said, "See that. He's a joker but he likes you. Inside, didn't you see the faces of the nieces and nephews? Even Hwang's daughters swooned as you recited from 'Azaleas.'"

"'Azaleas' is beautiful," said Sang-min. "Do you know the last two verses?"

"Of course," said Jae-wook and recited the third verse. "Step by step / on the flowers placed before you / tread lightly, softly as you go."

Sang-min recited the final verse. "When you leave / weary of me, / though I die, I'll not let one tear fall."

• • • •

DAYS SHORTENED AND morning earth frosted. Eun-mi chased the communal spirit for making winter kimchi, enlisting Kyung-wan and Hana to join her and Sang-min in soaking and pasting the cabbage leaves with salt and red pepper, and layering them in earthen jars. The days closed with cold hands, red faces, runny noses, and broad smiles. Sang-min worked at other chores to prepare for the great cold. Numerous trips to the hills with the back carrier and Kyung-wan filled the outbuilding with firewood. The remaining root crops were dug out and secured in a small cellar.

One morning near the end of November, Sang-min rose early, crossed the road, and washed in the cold waters of the spring. He put on a clean shirt, brushed his padded jacket, and departed for the village. The mourning period for Hwang had passed; the nephews wanted a parley.

Sang-min sat in a room in the Hwang compound with Jae-wook and the two nephews he'd seen before. Jae-wook said, "There are some concerns and it's best to speak frankly." The nephews nodded. "The family worries you might barge in where you know nothing and start giving orders, try to take over."

Sang-min shook his head. "I see my position as a student in the household."

The nephew who was a grocer laughed. "Well said. But let's talk about the woman."

"Eun-mi," said Jae-wook. "You can't be going back to see her. They don't want you following in old Hwang's footsteps. They want someone responsive to the business and faithful to Hyo-chu."

"I understand that," said Sang-min.

The grocer put a hand on Sang-min's back. "Hey, we're getting too serious. Let's get some food in here. Some soju."

Sang-min stayed until early evening. The children were asleep when he picked his way around the sharp corner, dropped down to the farm, and slid open the door to the second room. He sat in the dark feeling Eun-mi's eyes.

"I leave in the morning." There was much to do, he explained. Formal meetings. Tour the Hwang holdings. Learn their business ventures. Hyo-chu wanted a proper wedding with all preliminary ceremonies.

"Let's not talk about that now," said Eun-mi.

Sang-min shed his outer clothes, shed his long underwear, and slid under the blankets. Eun-mi touched his arm then his chest as she had so often. Sang-min turned to her and Eun-mi took him in coition with embraces and kisses. As the urgency increased and the point of withdrawal approached, Eun-mi said, "Ah, Sang-min, hold off. A little longer."

• • • •

IN THE MORNING, SANG-min and Eun-mi sat on the floor of the first room with Kyung-wan and Hana. Eun-mi put aside her chopsticks and clapped her hands.

She had an announcement: Sang-min was moving to the village to live with Hyo-chu and the Hwang family.

She had a small speech: through three seasons, from planting to harvest to winter kimchi, Sang-min had been friend and benefactor. Thanks to him, their root cellar and wood bin were full, and they had no fear of winter.

Hana interrupted with excitement in her voice. "You're going to live with Hye-su and the great Hwang family?"

Eun-mi lost the thread of her speech then fell to laughter. Sang-min laughed too but Kyung-wan tumbled his rice bowl and crossed to the door, sliding it open and bolting before Eun-mi could intervene.

"Well," she said, "that didn't go as planned. One has a tantrum and the other thinks you're marrying a chicken."

Eun-mi gathered the remains of the meal and scooted to the portico. Slipping into rubber shoes, she stepped down to the kitchen. Sang-min repaired to the second room to gather his knapsack and few belongings. He sat on the portico tightening the laces of his old combat boots, then stood, shouldered the knapsack, and walked toward the kitchen.

He looked about but saw no sign of Kyung-wan. Hana was running in circles, outside arm raised, inside arm down.

In the dimness of the kitchen, back to the doorway, Eun-mi tended the stove. Her shoulders heaved once, and Sang-min's right hand tightened on the knapsack strap.

"Sang-min," Eun-mi said without turning. "What? Are you still here? It's time to run along."

A Joke for Chong

Chong dives to a sprawl, flips on his back, rotates one-eighty, and drops feet first into our slit trench, grabbing his helmet on the way. Worthy of a silver medal. I maintain a squat outside the trench, not wanting to spill my half-heated water or drop the cigarette from my mouth. Also, I can differentiate between C-4 explosive and incoming artillery. Chong exits the trench with a grin as if to say, hey, just practicing. He points toward our rear, now our front, and says, aren't they supposed to yell fire in the hole? What are they doing anyhow?

I've figured out how to make a stove by punching holes in the bottom of an American C-ration can, filling it with twigs, and adding lighter fluid. I'm elated to see the water in my canteen cup at a roiling boil. Chong hovers above me, dirt embedded in his face, his hands, under his cracked fingernails. His armpits smell like half-dried ox shit, or is that me?

My guess, I say, they're blowing the bridge. And you're right, they should yell fire in the hole. What are they trying to do, scare us to death?

Chong says, so what good is blowing the bridge? Tanks can drive right through the stream.

I pry the lid off a can marked *coffee, instant, 1 oz net wt.*

Chong presses his argument. So why are we bothering with the bridge?

I look up from my squat. Chong, I say, do I resemble General Kim? Do you see stars on my shoulders?

Chong turns his face away and spits. He turns his face back, lowers it my way, and says in a confidential tone, you know, I'm not crazy about our current leadership.

He straightens his posture and says, what happened to Pak Jung-soo anyhow. When was he killed? How did it happen?

Poor Chong—his grasp of reality continues to deteriorate. I say, Pak wasn't killed. He was promoted.

Chong bends at the waist with his mouth open. Aar, aar, he says, that's a riot. He wasn't killed, he was promoted.

It's not a joke, I say. He was promoted and went to battalion staff.

Aar, aar, says Chong.

I remove the cigarette—which has burned to two centimeters—from my mouth, and sip instant coffee, *Hills Bros, Chicago, Ill*. Not bad. I light a fresh cigarette from the stub of the old one.

Chong has meandered down the trench line to second squad. I hear him bumbling through the tale of Pak's departure, ending with: he wasn't promoted, he was killed, aar, aar.

I clap a palm to my forehead. Chong, I call out, you idiot, you have it backwards.

Second squad laughs.

Class of '65

Never fired a round, I told Crawford. "Don't worry about it," he said. "You sure you know her by sight?"

We were between hootches back of the Blue Moon Club, an alleyway, hard-packed dirt, corrugated tin overhead, on either side platforms and sliding doors, inside each a square room, a working girl, a bed, a wardrobe. It was midday, not time for liberty, Crawford having cajoled a jeep and phony mission from the first sergeant. A few girls were about and beamed at Crawford, not me, not because I was black and he was white but because I was a specialist E-4 and he was a staff sergeant E-6. The girls knew their pay grades. One was in his face and I recognized her, hair dyed blond, folds clipped for the round-eye effect, older, thirties, worn out. Sergeant, she pitched, five dollar can do, good time.

"Hey," I said, "you know Lucy? Lucy, Eddie's yobo. Eddie, big guy. Blond like you." Yobo meant a steady girl, a sweetheart, paid by the month.

"Yeah I know. Why you want?" She led us a few doors down the alley and called out, "Yobosao. Soon-bok. Yobosao." Yobosao meant "hey." Soon-bok was Lucy's Korean name, her real name. The door to our front slid open. Eddie's yobo appeared in traditional wrap-around dress, not yet made up in mini-skirt and blouse. Like most of the girls, she kept her natural black hair and slanted eyes. Her nose flared and her skin color was closer to mine than Eddie's. Eddie was from the Midwest, Nebraska, North Dakota, somewhere, and was whiter than white. He liked to throw his arm over my shoulder because we were buddies, wouldn't happen back in the world, not in Nebraska or North Dakota, not even New Jersey, but it was okay, it felt good, I liked Eddie, and we would come into the ville together, that's how I knew his yobo.

Crawford said, "I don't know how to tell you. Eddie's dead." No reaction. He turned to blondie. "No understand?"

The two girls traded snatches of Korean. Blondie said, "So Eddie go home America. No take Soon-bok."

Crawford shook his head. "That's not it." He took the pose of a North Korean with a submachine gun. "Bap, bap, bap. Joe Chink. Eddie die in DMZ. Look, Eddie would want you to have this." He held out his right hand to Soon-bok. Military script: three tens and a five. And a gold ring with a blue stone, Eddie's class ring from high school. Soon-bok took the four pieces of script, the ring, and cried.

Two weeks later Crawford showed the squad a carbon copy of the incident report. We were in our barracks, the far quarter of a Quonset hut, cement floor, double bunks. The report was not accurate but Crawford said don't worry about it, that's the Army. That day the demilitarized zone—the four kilometers of no-man's land dividing the Koreas—was in late summer splendor, leaves thick, streams clear, sky blue, air savory, small deer and wild pigs skittery in the bush. No humans on our side but for foot patrols: olive fatigues, soft field hats, rifles, grenades. About forty meters south of the military demarcation line—the middle of the DMZ, the actual border between North and South Korea—our patrol had stopped. On the other side were six North Korean commandos in polished green, sneakers, submachines, mean mothers. Nothing separated us, the MDL being but a worn path.

The first lieutenant headed the patrol. Crawford was senior sergeant. One officer and twenty men. Crawford offered an opinion: why risk an incident? The lieutenant said because our mission was to assert our jurisdiction. Crawford offered a tactical suggestion: two teams, one goes up, one covers.

The lieutenant took the first team, which included Eddie and me, for a walk on the MDL, asserting our jurisdiction. What I remember next was him yelling, hit it. The incident report said the North Koreans shot first. I'm not sure. I did what the lieutenant said hugging the ground a meter south of the MDL. I looked up and Eddie was standing then fell backwards. The incident report said Eddie was returning fire but I don't think so, he just froze in place as the rest of us hit it. I lay there listening to the rattle of the submachine guns and the cracking of the covering team's return fire. Crawford paced behind the covering team—everyone else was on the ground—yelling aim those rifles, single shot, aim goddammit. Their scattered automatic bursts settled into rhythmic semi-automatic fire.

"Withdraw." My team reacted instantly to the lieutenant's order crawling and crouch running. "Not you." The lieutenant stopped me in mid-flight. "Hansson. Help me with Hansson." That was Eddie's last name. Later guys asked me if his eyes were open but I don't remember. I do remember two small holes in his flack vest—why do we wear those things if they don't stop a bullet?—with hints of blood.

We laughed at the estimate of hostile casualties. The incident report said we killed three and wounded two, absurd. Crawford, who had the best view, said maybe they took two hits as they withdrew in good order.

A few days later we were called to the command post, the lieutenant, Sergeant Crawford, me, at rigid attention, heels locked, hands at our sides, fingers curled, eyes and chins to the front, before the captain at his desk. The captain was pissed. The lieutenant had suggested we three be awarded bronze star medals, what was he thinking, why didn't he leave it alone?

"Is your name John Fucking Wayne?" the captain asked the lieutenant. "Answer me. Are you Lieutenant John Fucking Wayne?"

A petulant reply. "No sir."

His gaze moved to Crawford. "You, sergeant, are you John Fucking Wayne?"

Crawford answered with crisp immediacy. "No. Sir."

The captain's gaze moved to me. My hands trembled. I couldn't hold them still.

As we walked back to barracks, Crawford was in high humor. "That was easy. Just a good old ass chewing. 'Are you John Fucking Wayne?' The captain's funny."

I told Sergeant Crawford I was falling all over myself I was laughing so hard.

Crawford threw an arm over my shoulder, almost like Eddie used to. Loosen up, he urged.

Two days later the lieutenant came into our barracks to see Crawford. He called me over. He and Crawford sat on a bottom bunk. I sat on a foot locker. He offered cigarettes, Marlboro my favorite, and we lit up.

"It's been bad with the parents," the lieutenant said. "They keep writing to the captain asking what happened, how did he get killed, it's not Vietnam."

Short pause. "They're upset about his class ring. It wasn't with his effects. I thought we sent everything back."

Long pause. "Sir, you're not going to like this," said Crawford. "He lost it in a poker game. No idea where it is."

The lieutenant put his head in his hands. "Jesus Christ we can't tell them that."

"I agree," said Crawford.

The lieutenant looked up. "How are you guys doing?"

I don't remember answering. Maybe I nodded. Crawford said, "We're doing okay, sir. Thanks for asking."

Men at War

Darlene looks at her Mary Janes, brown with one strap. She folds her hands in her lap. Two sets of black leather shoes approach, spit shined. It kills Darlene that they wear military shoes with civvies, second lieutenants, no doubt, somewhere between officer candidate school and Vietnam. The one standing to her front complements his ebonies with tan slacks and blue dress shirt. Darlene rubs her left ring finger with thumb and forefinger from the other hand. Round and round. She raises her eyes and her peripheral catches Sally's pucker smile, blond bouffant, and pyramid breasts. Sally's soldier sounds like a cowboy from the Texas Panhandle.

"Couldn't help but notice y'all two charming ladies sitting here in desperate need of escorts."

Wide face, loose shoulders, blond buzz cut. Her soldier thin, brown hair an inch long, light gray military glasses, a half step behind his buddy. Sally takes to the banter like a puppy to Purina.

"If you all are asking us to dance, you all best do it before the music's over."

Texas gives a slight bow and extends a hand. Sally flicks eyebrows at Darlene and prances to her feet. Gray-glasses shifts weight from one leg to the other.

"May I?"

Darlene unfurls a smile and rises. *What's the point of coming out to the officers club to be a wet blanket? Then again, what's the point of coming out to the officers club?* On the dance floor, gray-glasses tightens the hand in the small of Darlene's back. This kills her too. Even the most timid pecker stirs at the scent of quarry. Darlene keeps her butt out and her face away from his, and they settle into a two-step. She raises her voice and talks over the horns from the band.

"What did you say?"

"Brad," he says. "My name's Brad."

Sally and Texas whir alongside as the horns climax. The boys grab a table and buy drinks. They're TAC officers at the Infantry OCS. Texas tells a story.

"So here we all are," he says, "on this hilltop after dark and one of the sergeants looks across to another hilltop and sees a fire. I mean like a brush fire. An actual fire."

Brad shakes his head and chuckles. Sally chuckles.

"So the sergeant yells, fire. And everyone looks at him. He yells, fire, fire. So they all start shooting their rifles. And he yells, no, goddamnit, a real fire, a real fire."

Brad and Texas push back in their chairs laughing. Sally laughs.

"Oh my god," she says, "that's such a riot. Darlene, powder room?"

The boys jump up as the girls exit. Sally takes Darlene's arm and spouts into one ear.

"Here's the deal," she says. "Your Brad has a car. I have a car. We're splitting up."

That might be Sally's deal, thinks Darlene.

"I'm not leaving here with Brad," she says.

They're in the wide hallway between the bathrooms. Sally stamps a foot.

"Don't spoil this for me," she says. She brushes four fingertips alongside Darlene's face. "And your hair. Why do you let it hang straight like that?"

"I'm not ready."

The foot trounces the carpet again.

"You don't have to—do anything. Just say good night and get out of the car—if that's what you want."

• • • •

A WARM GEORGIA NIGHT, starlight, midnight. Brad has a Chevy Impala, light green, with wide seats and an automatic transmission. It noses into a parking spot. Lights off. Motor off. Darlene stays on the passenger side close to the door. Brad looks across.

"I guess you're not inviting me in for a cup of coffee," he says.

Darlene pushes the door open and gains footing on the pavement. She swings the door shut and leans both elbows through the passenger window. Brad looks like a stray tabby. Darlene sighs.

"I want you to understand, Brad. You can come in but nothing's happening between us."

Brad jumps from the car and follows Darlene toward concrete outside stairs. Darlene glances back.

"Aren't you locking up?"

Brad scampers back to the Impala, rolls up windows, pushes locks, closes doors, and scampers back. Darlene climbs to the second level of the apartment complex, opens a front door into a living room, tosses a light switch, crosses to the kitchen, tosses another light switch. When she turns, Brad is staring at the eight-by-ten picture on the end table next to the couch, snapped twenty months before. In it, her left arm holds a man about the waist and his right arm encircles her shoulders. The man's hair is longer than Brad's, darker. No glasses. He wears a navy suit and her a pink dress, her lips deep red.

"My husband.""

Brad moves his eyes from the photo to Darlene then around the apartment. *There is not much to see*, thinks Darlene. No wall separating the living room and kitchen. A foyer-like hallway with doors for bedroom, bathroom, and linen closet. Brad's eyes are a soft brown. Another difference. The man in the picture has green eyes. The brown eyes return to Darlene and drop toward her left hand. She holds it up, knuckles out, fingers spread.

"Sally talked me into taking the rings off," she says.

"Where is he?"

"He's not anywhere, Brad."

But she shouldn't be flippant. Darlene squeezes her eyelids and tastes residue of ginger and rye. She opens her eyes.

"He died in Vietnam seven weeks ago."

Darlene doesn't take to the role of grieving widow. Wants to be the former grieving widow, that's it, the former grieving widow. She scoops coffee into the percolator basket. Pours water into the pot. Fires the stove as she listens to Brad.

"Wow. I mean, I'm sorry. I'm sorry to hear that."

Darlene opens an overhead cupboard. Cups and saucers jangle. The percolator slurps.

"Sally," Darlene says, "she's my best friend sort of. Our husbands were in the same OCS class."

A quart bottle of milk exits the refrigerator.

"They both got assigned here afterward. TAC officers just like you. One year here, off to Vietnam."

The coffee gurgles and settles.

"So Sally decided, you know, it was time I got out. Stopped feeling sorry for myself."

Brad says, "Is Sally a widow too?"

Darlene's first good laugh in a while rolls out. She takes the coffee pot off the stove and pours.

"Sally doesn't like to sit around."

Darlene sits in the chair across from Brad.

"I guess you wished you were the one with Sally," she says.

"I don't think so. I think I'd be in over my head."

Darlene can't tell if Brad's deadpan face is earnest or joking. She laughs her second good laugh in a while. Brad lowers his voice.

"Besides. I like you."

Oh Jesus.

"I like you too, Brad, but as I said, nothing's happening between us."

Brad stirs his coffee. He has an inquiry.

"Why is it you're still down here at Fort Benning?"

"Good question." Darlene sips at the edge of her cup and lowers it to the table. "I followed my husband down when he started OCS. An OC wife." Brad smiles. "Landed a job at the Infantry School, secretary, fifth floor. I can type like a bandit."

"So you're still here," says Brad.

"Still here."

Brad asks for the bathroom and Darlene moves to the living room, to the end of the couch near her husband's picture. James. Jim. Out of high school, Darlene had worked the Massachusetts high-tech belt through temp agencies, always got work, could type like a bandit. Used the family junker to commute. Turned twenty-one, stepped out to the bars, and met Jim, a senior at Boston University. She'd had other boyfriends. Larry, from high school, who worked at the Hi-Delite plant in Needham. Darlene wasn't catching the love vibes she thought she should with Jim but her mom told her, this one with the college, he's a keeper, forget about Larry the loser.

Jim graduated. They announced their engagement. Then he walked into a recruiting office and enlisted in the army. He'd be drafted anyway, he explained, and enlisting gave him a guaranteed shot at OCS. But a deferment, she said, he could get a deferment for marriage, for grad school, for teaching, for high-tech. Jim talked about duty, patriotism, communism, the domino theory, being a man. Darlene didn't get it. Here she was, investing her future in his smarts and this wasn't smart. Even Larry the loser had enough brains to flunk his induction physical.

The bathroom door opens and Brad meanders to the middle of the living room. Meanders toward the center of the couch. He sits. He edges closer and puts his right arm behind Darlene like he's stretching or enjoys the texture of couch fabric. His wrist drops against her shoulder and his coffee breath approaches. *What's wrong with his face? Ah, he's removed his glasses.* Darlene remembers her first impression of officer candidates at Fort Benning, marching, standing at attention, saluting, double-timing, rifles, steel helmets, bayonets; chests out, peckers in. They reminded her of her little brother and the neighborhood prepubescents playing war or cowboys and Indians. Bang, bang. Gotcha, you're dead. Didn't neither. Bang, bang.

Another memory. Two days before Jim left for Vietnam, they were driving off-base past a Dairy Queen, Darlene behind the wheel. At the outside window waiting for their soft-serves stood two men with beards and hair hanging past their shoulders. Men. Did you see that? Jim, did you see that? Jim laughed. Yeah, he said, they're hippies, they're all over the place now. Darlene had heard of hippies. So that's how they looked.

"Brad?"

"Um."

"Nothing below the neck. Okay? Those are the rules."

Brad's brown eyes widen. Darlene absorbs the pressure of his hand behind her neck and his lips against hers. Reminds her of Jim in the beginning, not a great kisser either. Larry was a great kisser. But a loser.

Jim's family lived north of Detroit. High-salary white-collar job in the auto industry. Could afford to fly to the wedding, rent a car, stay at the Boston Park Plaza, hoity toity. Nothing wrong with hoity toity, said Darlene's mom. After the wedding, after basic training, after OCS, after going over, after the notification team left the apartment, Darlene stood at the wall phone and dialed Jim's mom. They agreed his remains should return to his childhood home north of Detroit and Darlene drove there for the funeral. She listened to rifles and taps and prayers and clasped a triangle of American flag which she passed to her mother-in-law.

Brad's left hand drops along the front of Darlene's blouse past the collar bone. Darlene pushes it back up to her shoulder. He doesn't try again. An obedient soldier. One minor infraction. At the funeral reception, Darlene felt her mother-in-law's gaze. Was she angry about the flag? Wasn't that the right thing to do? Then Darlene understood. She was checking for a four-month tummy bulge. Sorry, mom. She pushes a palm against Brad's chest and makes light with her voice.

"Slow down, lieutenant."

She rises from the couch and pulls Brad by the hands. He talks about seeing her again, about a phone number. She removes his glasses from his shirt pocket, places them on his face, leads him to the door. A short kiss.

"It's been a nice night, Brad."

Another short kiss. A nudge. He's across the threshold, turning away, looking back, descending the stairs. The Impala motor starts and its headlamps sweep a quarter circle as the car backs into the street. Darlene douses the outside light. The living room light. Crosses to the kitchen and washes the coffee cups. She wonders if Brad will have sex before he dies and sighs. Not her problem.

Darlene locates her spiral notebook in the pull-out drawer next to the stove and takes it to the kitchen table. She clicks open a blue ballpoint and cocks her elbow. *Dear Sir*, she writes, *I cannot begin to tell you how much I've enjoyed working at the Infantry School. I will never forget the kindness your section showed me after——*.

Darlene rips out the page and crumples it. She reapplies her cocked elbow. *Dear Sir, It is with regret that I inform you of my resignation from your——*.

Darlene crumples another page. She wonders what she'll do. The thought of going back to Massachusetts depresses her. The thought of going anywhere depresses her. Maybe she'll go to San Francisco and join the hippies. Maybe she'll just get in the car and drive and drive.

Dear Sir.

Low Speed Jet

A whisper so the men wouldn't hear, the column halted at the ready, facing out, squatting, staring into sawgrass, rifles leveled, grenade launchers angled. Our helmets touched.

"Nick, what the fuck are you doing?"

"Ah'm leading my platoon, Dag, what are y'all doing?"

What was I all doing? Not what I wanted with five weeks left in-country, but the new battalion commander—a new one every four months—had a brainstorm: staff officers with field experience mentoring new lieutenants.

"Nick, don't go out ahead. That's what your point man's for."

"Dag, sometimes you gotta get out front. At Fort Benning—"

"Forget Fort Benning. If you trip a booby or take a sniper, then what? No more platoon leader."

Nick lifted the corners of his mouth, likable no matter how dumb he behaved. He moved away, turning once to say, ah'm good, and resumed his place at the front of the column. Behind the point. Two nights later he found my sandbagged, half-buried officers quarters. Ducked in with a bottle of Jim. We sat on a cot, dragged out canteen cups, and sipped. He apologized for being a dick. I said it was okay. The whiskey took hold. On the transistor, Armed Forces Radio sent us *Sweet Little Sixteen*. Nick bobbed his shoulders. Surprised me.

"You like Chuck Berry?"

Nick had blond hair cut to a flattop and a round face on a six-foot frame, which he moved closer.

"Ah like 'em all."

He poured more whiskey. I waved a forefinger.

"Look, Nick, you don't wanna get killed in this shit hole. Stay off the point. Blend in with the men. Don't look like the leader."

I tried to think of another exhortation. Nick pulled my hand down.

"Dag, we're all going sometime. What's better? Dying in bed at eighty? Or a military funeral with the trimmings? All your friends there."

"But Nick, here's the problem, you're not around to see that grand funeral. You're the guy in the box."

"I'll see it aforehand."

Nick wobbled to his feet and slapped his breast.

"Heah I am taking a bullet."

He staggered a step back.

"But in my last gasp I see it all. The honor guard, the three-gun salute, the bugler. Just like fucking Arlington."

He dropped to the cot.

"Then ah expire, a happy warrior."

"Nick, you gotta take this shit serious."

"Hot damn, Dag, we've killed half this bottle."

He leaned into me, wrapped an arm, and cupped my far shoulder.

"Don't fret, ol' buddy. Whatever happens, it'll be alright. It'll be A-okay."

• • • •

I ROTATED BACK TO FORT Benning with captain's bars and a desk job at the Infantry School. I asked my section commander about my career path. He told me the war was winding down. I rented an apartment off-base and wrote letters of inquiry to law schools. I bought a red '67 Mustang with a 289 V8 and forty thousand on the odometer. Went for rides in the Georgia countryside. Sometimes I crossed the Chattahoochee and cruised Alabama. The Mustang began stalling. One of my sergeants went under the hood with a screwdriver, tried a few carburetor adjustments.

"Sorry, sir, I think it's your low speed jet."

"What's that?"

"It pulls in the fuel when your foot's off the gas."

"It can't be fixed?"

"You should really spring for a new carb, sir."

"Jesus, forty thousand miles."

Next day a telegram entered my in-box. Unusual. I turned it about several times. It was from my old battalion commander letting me know that Nick had tripped a booby. Wanted to let me know before I saw his name on the back pages of the *Army Times*. He asked if I'd represent the battalion since Nick's home was near Fort Benning, less than eighty miles.

I wore my dress greens, Vietnam Service Medal, Combat Infantryman Badge. The graveside had a good turnout, dark suits, black dresses, black skirts, pants suits, jeans with windbreakers, green work pants, bib overalls. The honor guard pulled up in a blue sedan, three airmen, semi-polished shoes. Airmen? They pulled rifles and a cassette player from the trunk. When their turn came, the lead airman called ready, aim, and they fired their blanks. Ready, aim, a second time. Ready, aim, the last time with one rifle empty. The lead airman pressed a button on the cassette player. They presented arms. Seconds of dead air and a recording of taps scratched my ears.

The farm house and barn looked just like Nick said. I wandered room to room, talked to siblings, cousins, school chums, clutched fried chicken and potato salad. Nick's cousin Bella Anne shadowed me.

"You coming into town with us all, Captain D'Agostino?"

She winked.

"Where we can get some proper refreshment."

I told her thanks but I had to get back to my men at Fort Benning. I found Nick's mom for the goodbye. She hugged me. She told me how much it meant, me coming to the service. She produced a letter in Nick's scrawl. I saw my name and good buddy in the same sentence. I glanced around for Nick's dad.

"Pap's in the barn. Chores won't wait."

Pap sat on a one-legged stool squeezing the tits of a black and white Guernsey, streams of milk tingling and frothing the stainless steel pail underneath. Behind him lounged a brown Jersey. I knew about the cows because Nick had told me, joking about the Jersey being my home state. Pap's suit jacket hung on a wooden peg and he wore coveralls over pants and shirt, necktie still in place. He looked up but didn't lose a stroke. I pushed my toe into straw and sawdust.

"I'm real sorry about Nick."

"Y'all take care."

I twisted the key and the 289 went into a rough lope. Gas down, clutch up. Second gear, third. Thirty on the dirt road, swirls of dust in the rear view mirror. Thoughts went to that ass, my former battalion commander, he didn't have to tell me. I didn't look at the back pages of the *Army Times* anymore, never would have known, would have gone the rest of my life seeing Nick not blown to shit. And that crappy funeral detail. Not even Army. Scruffy shoes, canned taps. Couldn't present arms without a slouch. Couldn't wait to fold the flag and clear out.

The dirt road came upon a stop sign. As fuel intake switched to the low speed jet, the motor sputtered and stalled. I raised my right hand, formed a fist, and pounded the top of the steering wheel. The wheel flexed and my fist bounced up. This piece of shit, this fucking piece of shit. Forty thousand miles and falling apart. I pounded again. Fucking shit, you hear me, mother fucking shit. Worthless, goddam nothing. I looked in the rear view mirror. I looked up and down the abutting tar road. Nobody around. My eyes felt wet, my nose too. Jesus Christ, a captain of infantry going bullshit over a junk carburetor. I turned the key, pressed the gas, let out the clutch. Forty, fifty miles per hour, high gear. I turned the radio tuner. No, don't want no gospel. No, no country. Chuck Berry came on, *Johnny Be Good*. Go, Johnny, go.

Wait a minute. Nick never knew about that crappy funeral detail. He only knew what he saw in the second after tripping the booby. He would have felt the tug of the wire, figured what was coming. And in that instant he would have seen what every warrior's heart wants, a spit-shined honor guard, Army, ramrod straight, a real bugler. Just like fucking Arlington. So it's alright. It's A-okay.

Government Issue

Leon and Mee-yung took a stroll, mid-April 1968. Mee-yung belonged to Leon, his yobo, his sweetheart, for thirty dollars per month. Leon belonged to the US Army, drafted at eighteen, shipped over at nineteen, but Korea that year, even near the DMZ, was better than the other place, the hell-pit, Vietnam. And Leon didn't grunt hills with rifle and grenade but worked for a transport section. Regular hours with evenings in the ville, that medley of mud and stick hooches squatting by and enveloping the khaki-draped military compound. Hey GI whatcha want? Dirty movie blow job five dollar. Three dollar can do. Hey GI.

The couple meandered the dirt paths rippling from the roadway that split the ville. They passed clusters of hooches, looked out on rice paddies, meandered back. At one of the clusters, an L-shaped enclave of abutting rooms and sliding doors, five GI's, all white, sat on the narrow veranda, drinking, talking, laughing, their girls standing nearby gabbing in Korean. Leon recognized Jimmy Noyes from his section, also a specialist fourth class, a dispatcher, kept books, calculated loads, plotted routes. Jimmy called out, holding a can of Bud, pointing, beckoning. The other guys waved, yeah, c'mon over.

Leon didn't have a problem with white guys. The off-duty drift tended toward segregation but guys who knew each other crossed over. Mee-yung – she had a problem with white guys, or rather with white guys' girls. It seemed droll to Leon that prejudice ran deeper for the working girls, whether they serviced brothers or not, than among the GI's themselves. Inside the low walls, the claque of mini-skirts gave Mee-yung the once over, thin smiles, went back to their chatter. Mee-yung tugged Leon's sleeve but he ignored her – here was something to do, to kill the afternoon. He pushed into the courtyard and closed a hand around the Bud.

Jimmy said, "Leon drives an M49."

This impressed the white guys. Not that Leon cared. He was a big kid with oversize feet and hands that dwarfed his cuffs. He had a chestnut face with straight nose and lips that rolled out.

"Yeah I carry diesel up to first and third."

Shit, man, across the river? The DMZ?

"Uh huh but I worry most about this side. The kids."

Kids?

"They run out in the road. If they go under a rear wheel you wouldn't even feel it." Leon tipped the Bud, brought it down. "I go real slow through the ville."

Well, Jesus Christ, they got every fucking thing in the road here, mamasans, papasans, bicycles. Ox carts. Another GI said, yeah, run a few over and they'll get their shit together. The white guys laughed except one who said, you fucking nuts? You wanna end up in a gook jail?

Jimmy said, "The Korean courts can't touch you if you're on duty." He pulled on his cigarette and exhaled. "It would stay military. It would go to a court-martial."

Leon said, "Guys, I don't want none of that. No Korean jail. No court-martial. No nothing. Maybe another beer."

The white guys laughed. Right on. Fucking A.

Mee-yung stood next to Leon ignoring the white guys' girls who time to time tossed her a pout or wrinkled nose or ass wiggle. In the shade of the veranda, the air cooled. The GI's drifted to the center of the courtyard, felt the sun, felt the buzz of the beer. Leon thought it one of his better Sundays in the ville.

• • • •

TUESDAY MORNING, LEON sat in the company mess with toast and scrambled eggs. Bacon, coffee, orange juice. His favorite military meal. Jimmy appeared kitty-corner with a cup of coffee.

"Hey that was great. Sunday. That's your yobo then? Nice. You taking her back?"

It crossed soldiers' minds, taking their yobos back to the world. Leon had daydreamed of them settling in, him and Mee-yung, a second-floor apartment on Kirkwood Ave in South Atlanta, a baby, everyone coming around, admiring his exotic wife. It would be something. He wondered if his grandmother would like her. Ask her what she did in Korea.

Leon said, "I wouldn't know how to start doing that."

"It's not hard. There's places in the ville – they can set you up. Marriage license, visa. Plane ticket. All you need is money."

Leon laughed and scooped some scrambled egg.

"Not much," said Jimmy. "A thousand or so."

"Out of sight."

Jimmy leaned forward. "Maybe not."

Leon knew Jimmy did payday loans, parceling out two-dollar disbursements to needy GI's the last week of the month, collecting three the week following. He'd also heard that Jimmy erased equipment from the books and sold it in the ville. There were jokes about Jimmy Minderbinder and J&J Enterprises.

Leon said, "I'm looking to stay out of trouble."

"Me too. Look. Leon. Try it once. If you don't like it, forget it."

A half hour later, Leon signed out his M49 A2C Tank Truck from the motor pool and stood by at the fuel depot as the crew pumped 1200 gallons of diesel into the rear-mounted main tank. Jimmy pulled up in an open jeep. Leon mounted the cab of the truck, engaged the transmission, and paraded behind Jimmy through the compound gate into the ville. He sat high shifting gears, revving the motor, the jeep a blot to his front, crawling, just the right speed. At the end of the ville, Jimmy ticked up the speed.

Three kilometers out, paddies and river on the left, thin woods on the right, the jeep slowed, right signal blinking. As it turned, Jimmy twisted and looked up at the truck's windshield. Leon slowed, down-shifted, down-shifted again, hesitated, then wound the steering wheel clockwise. They crept along a narrow side road, little more than a double path, soon opening to a scattering of hooches. At Jimmy's hand signals, Leon reversed the rig and backed between two hooches. The rear-view mirrors showed Korean civilians lined up with five-gallon jerrycans.

Leon heard the gravity hose run out, felt diesel leaving the main tank like blood from his veins. In ten minutes, Jimmy sat alongside tucking military script, two twenties, into Leon's hand.

"Jimmy, how much did you take?"

"A hundred gallons."

"You're shitting me."

"It's nothing."

Jimmy pointed to the clipboard on his lap. It held a requisition form identical to the one on Leon's clipboard. Only the new form read 1100 instead of 1200. Leon's eyes dropped to the signature box – Lieutenant Cox – same as the original.

"We'll never get away with this," said Leon. "The lieutenant's not stupid."

"The lieutenant signs anything put in front of him."

They swapped forms.

"He's gonna catch on."

"He's in on it," said Jimmy.

"What?"

"Leon, you think I could of done this myself?" Jimmy pushed a shoulder against Leon's. "You worry too much. Look, twice a week, no more. A whiff of trouble, we stop."

• • • •

NEXT PAYDAY EVENING, Leon and Mee-yung sat cross-legged on the linoleum floor of her cubby-hole back of the Blue Moon Tea

House. Leon placed a twenty-dollar note between them followed by a ten. Mee-yung smiled, thank you, yobo.

"Wait." Leon blocked her hand, savoring the moment, watching her face as he dropped a second twenty.

But Mee-yung didn't squeal and clap as Leon anticipated. She tightened her lips. "Where you get money?"

Leon took her hands. "Mee-yung, you wanna go America?"

"All yobo wanna go America. Where you get money?"

"You no understand."

"Yeah understand. Where you get?"

"Mee-yung, yobo, you know Jimmy?" Leon pointed in the direction of the hooches they had stopped by that April day. He lifted his hand in a drinking motion. Beers. White GI's.

Mee-yung nodded. "Yeah know Jimmy. Slicky boy."

"No," said Leon. "No slicky boy."

Mee-yung dropped her head.

Leon said, "Three months, four months, *tacsan* money. No wanna go America?"

Mee-yung pointed to her transistor radio, a scratched-up Sony, light gray with jutting silver antennas. The girls loved their American pop and Korean soap. Leon often watched them sighing to crackling dialogue.

"All a time GI gonna take yobo America. All a time break heart."

"No," said Leon. "No break heart."

• • • •

ONE MORNING TOWARD the end of June, Leon sat in the high tanker cab, transmission in neutral, motor idling, glancing at rear view mirrors filled with jerrycans and Koreans, diesel flowing. It had settled into routine. Twice a week, forty dollars per trip, eighty dollars per week, easy money. But on this early summer day, from Leon's left, from the double path that led to the main road, came a villager knees pumping, arms waving crosswise over his head. As he passed the truck, Leon went to the mirrors and saw Korean backsides in flight across the berms of the rice paddies.

Leon turned his gaze frontward. From the double path flowed a file of jeeps marked Military Police. Their occupants wore black armbands and helmet liners bearing the letters MP in white letters. As from a box seat, best in the house, Leon watched the MP's dismount, spread out, surround Jimmy, take photos, write on clipboards. A major yelled orders.

The tanker's passenger door opened and an MP climbed in. To Leon's left, the major stepped on the running board and pushed a clipboard through the window. A disciplinary report, he said, sign at the bottom. The major handed Leon a carbon copy and jumped down.

"Let's go," said the MP. Leon looked at him. The MP explained. Leon was to complete his delivery, return the truck to the motor pool, and report to his commanding officer.

Leon engaged the transmission, drove to the main road, turned right, geared up, gave a sideways look. "What's gonna happen?"

"All I can say, buddy, is you're in a world of shit."

• • • •

LEON STOOD BEFORE THE sign, Judge Advocate General. The previous month had floated half-real starting with his commanding officer gaping at the discipline report, saying, "Jesus," then, "You're confined to quarters." Quarters meant barracks, latrine, mess hall, and work, now the motor pool, no longer driving the big rig. There were no passes to the ville. Leon conversed with Mee-yung through a translation service. He sent money. She sent endearments, still his yobo, hoping for the best, that he would soon be free. Then he'd been ordered to report to JAG at division headquarters. A general court-martial had been convened with Leon on the docket.

Leon passed the JAG sign, ascended a gravel path, and stopped between two Quonset huts. The one on the right said Court and appeared empty. Leon turned to the hut on the left. It overflowed with desks, chairs, and clerks. Paperwork everywhere, in manila folders, on clipboards, stapled, clipped, loose. A clerk led Leon to a small office with one desk, two chairs, and behind the desk a thin man, late twenties, with blond hair and light-gray military glasses. The collar of his dress khakis held two silver bars and his nameplate read Captain Jacob Shapiro. Leon stood to attention.

Shapiro waved Leon to a chair. "Specialist Davis," he said, "I'm your defense attorney. You can talk freely with me." Shapiro read the charge, misappropriation of government property, to wit, selling government fuel to Korean civilians. "I tried to get this knocked down to a special. Since your accomplice ..." Shapiro thumbed through papers. "Ah, yes, your accomplice, Specialist James Noyes, got off with a summary."

Leon had not seen Jimmy since the day they were caught. He'd heard that the military police held him for a few days then transferred him to a unit at division headquarters. Special, Leon knew, meant special court-martial, not as serious as his general. Jimmy's summary court-martial would have been less serious still, a one-officer affair.

Leon said, "What happened with Specialist Noyes, sir?"

"He ... let me see, here, he got off pretty light. Considering the offense. Here it is. Demoted one grade to private first class, confined to quarters for sixty days, extra duty for forty-five days. Forfeiture of two-thirds pay for two months."

Shapiro looked up. "He turned state's evidence. He put the finger on ... on the ring leader. First Lieutenant Edward Cox."

"What happened with Lieutenant Cox, sir?"

"It's happening. General court-martial same as you. Him first, then you. Noyes will be testifying against him."

"I could turn state's evidence," said Leon.

"Really?"

"Yessir, Noyes told me all about Lieutenant Cox."

Shapiro slipped down in his chair and shook his head. "Sorry. Hearsay."

"What do we do, sir?"

"We'll plead guilty. Concentrate on the punishment phase."

Leon felt his lower lip sag.

"Specialist Davis, you were caught red-handed."

Got me there, thought Leon.

"Look," said Shapiro, "who can vouch for your character? Platoon leader? Platoon sergeant?"

"Sergeant Dumont. My section chief."

Shapiro scribbled on a yellow pad. "Good, good, anyone else?"

Leon looked past Shapiro. "Maybe my yobo."

"Be right back," said Shapiro. Five minutes later, he returned with a Korean in slacks and short-sleeve shirt. "This is Mr. Kim. Our Korean liaison and translator."

"How long have you had this yobo?" said Kim. "You still paying her? She still your yobo?"

Kim turned to Shapiro. "She'll make a good witness. She can say how much she loves him, wants to marry him. All that stuff. We'll pay her some expenses." Leon told Kim where Mee-yung lived. Kim scribbled Korean characters in a small notebook and left.

"What will they give me, sir?" said Leon.

"The court can do anything. The max, now don't get excited, the max is five years at Leavenworth. Forfeiture of pay, dishonorable discharge." Leon felt his eyes water. "But that won't happen. That's just the max. I'm hoping they'll let you off with a few months. Here, in the Eighth Army stockade, that would be nice. Bad time but no dishonorable." Shapiro paused. He pushed the bridge of his glasses. "Okay? We've got two weeks to prepare."

• • • •

THE SECOND DAY OF COX'S court-martial, early morning, Leon sat in Shapiro's office. He'd been there the day before, waiting, not knowing when Cox would end and he'd start. Two men with JAG insignia appeared in the doorway, one large and balding with a paunch and the silver eagle of a full colonel, the other a captain, Shapiro's age, black hair. Shapiro walked to the doorway and they chatted.

Shapiro resumed his seat behind the desk. "Lieutenant Cox flew in a civilian lawyer from the States. Ripped Noyes apart yesterday on cross. And those phony requisitions ..." Leon nodded. The lieutenant's signature was all over them. They had him there. "Cox signed hundreds of requisitions a week. Depended on the enlisted men to keep him straight. That civilian lawyer, he's walking all over us."

"Who were those officers, sir?"

"The colonel's in charge of our JAG section." Shapiro explained that he sat as the military judge on courts-martial. The captain was prosecuting Cox. "He'll be your prosecutor too."

"If Lieutenant Cox gets off, that's good for us, right, sir?"

"No it's bad." Shapiro drummed a pen on the desk. "The court, they'll be in a foul mood, they don't like not guilty. Then we walk in." Shapiro jumped up. "Hang easy. I'm gonna check on Cox."

At 1100, Shapiro reappeared scooping folders from his desk. "They're done. We're on."

"Lieutenant Cox?"

"Not guilty. Vote was six to three. The colonel wants to knock off your guilt phase before lunch."

"Sir?"

"They have to hear you plead guilty and vote on it. It won't take long. After lunch we'll do the punishment."

Leon and Shapiro entered the courtroom. At a small table on the right sat the thick-bodied JAG colonel. To the left, at one of two larger tables, sat Leon's prosecutor, the black-haired captain. Leon and Shapiro marched straight ahead to face nine infantry officers sitting behind a semicircle of tables. Shapiro saluted the central figure, a colonel with wide face and red crew cut. Leon felt himself nudged to the defense table.

Shapiro announced a plea of guilty. The JAG colonel asked Leon to confirm the plea. Then everyone except the officers on the semicircle scraped back chairs and filed outside. Five minutes later, Shapiro and Leon again stood facing the semicircle. The red-haired colonel pronounced the court's finding, guilty, and they recessed for lunch.

• • • •

AT 1330, THE COURT reassembled. Shapiro said, "The defense calls Lee Mee-yung."

Mee-yung entered the Quonset hut in traditional wrap-around dress and bunned hair with comb. Mr. Kim, in suit and tie, followed and stood next to the witness chair. Shapiro approached.

"Do you know the defendant, Specialist Leon Davis?" Mee-yung listened to Kim's translation, raised her eyelids an instant, lowered them.

"*Ye*," she said.

"Yes," said Kim.

"Could you tell the court the nature of your relationship?"

They were planning to marry, Mee-yung said. They were in love. More open-ended questions. Mee-yung replied with voice low, eyes down, Kim providing amplification as well as English.

"At some point," said Shapiro, "did you become aware of a soldier known as Jimmy?" Mee-yung's eyes remained down but her voice rose in pitch. Yes, he was an instigator, a smooth operator, the source of Leon's misdeeds.

Leon tried to catch Mee-yung's gaze. Her eyelashes rose but for the barest second.

Leon glanced sideways at his adjudicators, colorless faces in semicircle of nine. They might just as well have been viewing soldiers marching on parade or dead in trenches.

Shapiro had stopped asking questions. The black-haired captain said, "No cross."

Leon watched Mee-yung walk to the door and out.

Sergeant Dumont entered in dress khakis, short-sleeve shirt, arms and face of ebony, two rows of ribbons over his left pocket. He saluted the court and took the witness chair, sitting at attention.

"Do you know the defendant, Specialist Leon Davis?" Shapiro asked.

"One of my best men. Sir."

Leon looked from witness chair to military judge to prosecutor to court of nine and back to the witness chair. Shapiro had just asked if Leon – "hypothetically, now" – were punished with time in the stockade – "not discharged," would Dumont be willing to take him back?

"In a heartbeat. Sir."

Shapiro finished his examination. The black-haired captain had no cross. Dumont rose, saluted the court, and made his about-face. Shapiro returned and sat next to Leon.

The JAG colonel nodded. Shapiro rose. "Colonel. Gentlemen. We all make mistakes. Sometimes we make bad mistakes. That doesn't mean we should be tossed on the scrap heap."

Shapiro talked for five minutes.

The black-haired captain rose. "The prosecution requests ..." He looked down at his papers. "Uh, punishment, commensurate with the offense."

Chairs scraped. Leon and the JAG colonel and the captains and the court clerk stepped outside. Ten minutes later, the door to the Quonset hut opened and a hand beckoned. Cigarettes were pinched, smoke exhaled, places taken. Leon and Shapiro approached the court and stood at attention. The red-haired colonel spoke as the remaining eight looked on.

Leon concentrated on keeping the proper position of attention, hands curled, not trembling, shoulders back, head level, eyes ahead, and at the end about-facing without falter. He felt awareness of eyes and mouths widening but not until he stood outside with Shapiro, Shapiro's fists clenched, face blanched, did the red-haired colonel's words enter his consciousness, that he was to be reduced in rank to private, imprisoned for five years, forfeit all pay, and be dishonorably discharged.

Shapiro took Leon's arm. "The commanding general will review this. He'll knock it down." Shapiro looked around. "This is so fucked even for the army."

Leon said, "What do I do now, sir?"

"You have to report to the Eighth Army stockade. Tomorrow."

"What about Mee-yung, sir?"

"What?"

"Can I talk to her?"

"Private Davis. That's over."

• • • •

NEXT MORNING, LEON rode south in the back of an open jeep, Dumont right front with a forty-five caliber pistol. "Regulations," he said. "For transporting a prisoner." Soon the jeep traipsed center Seoul with its agglomeration of foot traffic, mini-buses, military jeeps, trucks, bicycles, ox carts, a few cars, and on the opposite outskirt entered a compound of chained link fence topped by spirals of barbed wire. Eighth Army Disciplinary Barracks.

Leon shouldered his duffel and with Dumont passed on foot through two wide gates to a cinder-block building of pallid green. There he emptied his duffel on the floor to the orders of a three-stripe sergeant, stripped, leaned forward against a wall, turned his face, opened his mouth.

"Spread 'em," said the sergeant. He looked. He told Leon to dress and turned to Dumont. "You can go."

Dumont looked like he wanted to say something. His lips moved. Then he was gone.

A specialist wearing an MP helmet liner stood at the door. The sergeant said, "Go with him. Leave your shit here."

The MP brought Leon to attention and issued orders. Forward march, left turn march, right turn march. The MP marched in step to Leon's left rear and pattered in his ear. "We're seeing the commandant. He's gonna rip you a new asshole. Just stand at attention and take it."

And: "Don't say a thing unless I flick my eyes. Then say yessir real smart like."

The MP brought Leon to a halt at a wide set of steps leading to a porch. The porch fronted a normal house, not cinder block, not a Quonset hut. It might have been his grandmother's house in South Atlanta.

They went up the steps and entered a foyer. The MP put Leon at attention and followed suit facing him at two meters. Minutes later a tall man with thin nose and brown hair entered to Leon's peripheral.

"Sir," said the MP. "Prisoner Davis."

The commandant approached so his breath touched Leon's right ear.

"You know why you're here?" said the commandant. The MP's eyes held steady. "Because you're fucking scum."

The commandant walked to Leon's left ear.

"Do you understand that, prisoner?"

The MP flicked his pupils.

"Yessir," said Leon.

"I got a letter," said the commandant. He held a typed piece of paper in front of Leon's face. "From a JAG captain. Shapiro. He says you're a sweet boy."

Outside Leon resumed position to the right front of the MP. They marched not toward the in-processing building but a larger one-story square of green cinder.

More patter. "You're gonna be here a few days. You're not gonna like it. Keep your cool."

A narrow hallway ran the inside perimeter of the building. Another specialist led them a quarter way around, lifted a bolt, and dragged open a steel door, solid except for a small, barred window. Leon crossed the threshold and heard behind him a yawn and a scrape.

Leon's pupils adjusted to the darkness. He saw he was in a cell less than two meters wide of dank cinder block, the floor a cement slab. He took a step in and stopped at the apparition of a pale face on the back wall, not far, the cell being less than three meters in length.

"Stay away from me, nigger," said the face.

The pale prisoner's hands came up sideways as in hand-to-hand combat.

Leon thought, I could snap that little cracker's neck with one hand. Both men breathed in gasps. Leon stepped back, to the door, lowered his heartbeat, let his pupils dilate. There was nothing in the cell – no bunk, no stool, no blanket, nothing – except the two prisoners and what they wore. Leon brought his hands to his face. The shame. Disciplinary barracks, a dishonorable discharge, his parents, his grandmother, friends from high school.

At the end of day two, Leon blinked in gathering twilight. From latrine privilege, he had been led outside. He followed an MP to a Quonset hut, a standard barracks with bunks, tin wall lockers, wooden foot lockers. Guys looked up from reading, playing cards, shooting the shit. The MP said, "Keep your nose clean."

At the end of day nine, Leon received a summons from the guard shack, a white wood-frame rectangle. The duty sergeant pointed toward the far end. Captain Shapiro, holding a briefcase, staring at the floor, lifting his eyes at Leon's approach.

"How are they treating you?"

"It was little rough at first, sir."

"We got your sentence knocked down to eighteen months. Still Leavenworth. You'll be flown back in a few days."

"Still a dishonorable, sir?"

"With good behavior, you'll be out in a year. But, yeah, still a dishonorable. Look, I'm writing a letter to the commandant at Leavenworth."

"Don't do that, sir."

"What?"

"Please don't, sir. They don't like letters from JAG."

Shapiro ran his tongue between his lips.

Leon looked past the captain out the guard shack door. He peered across the Pacific Ocean, the Rocky Mountains, the High Plains, past Fort Leavenworth. He tried to see Georgia.

"Sir, that letter. Could you write it to my grandmother?"

"Say again?"

"I can't tell her, sir. You're good at explaining things."

Shapiro blinked. "Sure." He pitched his voice higher. "Absolutely." He dragged a yellow pad from his briefcase. "I can do that."

Rearguard

Jana backed off from Barry's fart. No odor but a blast, a massive rip that blossomed the seat of his Royal Robbins convoy shorts before undulating out a leg hole. Okay, maybe she imagined the blossoming and undulating, but not the acoustics. Barry, a meter ahead, uphill, his left boot perched on a stone set in the trail for that purpose, twisted his body and said, "Sorry." A wide tan hat protected his balding pate and shadowed the mien of sincerity on his salt and pepper face.

"Quite alright," said Jana. "Some things can't be helped. I suppose."

Barry turned, applied hiking poles to path, and lifted his right foot. Jana let him gain several steps, and several steps later he ripped another, his head making a half turn and his shoulders shrugging. Oh, thought Jana, why did I sign up for this? But answered her own question, for an overseas adventure on the cheap, airfare her only expense. In exchange, she helped Mike with logistics and co-led the hikes, working the sweep position. She let Barry get ahead a few more steps.

The trail leveled and entered a stand of thin hardwood. Barry stopped, dropped his pack, and unzipped an outer pocket. He glanced up from his bent-over rummaging and said, "Afraid I need a bio break."

Jana put forefinger and middle finger to her lips and cast a sharp whistle. As Barry tucked in his head, the eleven hikers ahead stopped and turned.

"Tell Mike we'll be delayed," said Jana.

Sound waves rippled to the front of the group and back. Number eleven, a stocky blond, turned, and said with New York elocution, "Can't it wait ten minutes?"

Jana said, "Doesn't look like it."

Sound waves again rippled up and back, and number eleven said, "Okay, we'll wait for you at the next trail junction, but try to make it snappy." The front eleven resumed their march.

Barry entered the hardwoods, trail right, clutching a quart baggie of toilet paper. He paused mid-step and said, "You can go on. I'll catch up."

Jana shook her head. "You know I can't. I'm the sweep." Barry disappeared into the trees.

Jana took assigned responsibilities with their deserved seriousness. Her job as sweep entailed, if nothing else, security: to be the last one through, to make sure nobody wandered off trail, to alert Mike of any issues—an injury, an equipment failure, an urgent call of nature.

She leaned on her poles and peered rearward. On in-and-out hikes, rearward glances helped with trail recognition coming out. On any hike, they alerted the group to happenings from behind, such as overtaking trekkers, or animals.

Jana leaned further over her poles. A four-legged critter, tan in color, head down, ears up, had emerged at the last bend in the trail. As the animal approached, Jana confirmed its species: a canine, a domesticated dog, a lab, she decided, it being hefty but not a shepherd or collie. The animal stopped and lifted a back leg—a male lab.

Jana advanced a step, putting herself between the dog and Barry's pack, between the dog and her group. She knew that vagabond dogs in foreign countries posed danger, not so much of attack, but disease. They carried insects and harbored viruses. They could scratch and nip and emit fluids. When they approached a group, people could not resist reaching out a hand or bending from the waist.

Dogs back home were different, pampered, picked up after, neutered, immunized, bathed. The couple in the next apartment had a terrier, no children but a terrier. Jana recalled the day they brought it home, over eleven years ago, ringing her bell, double smiles from the hallway, the puppy giving a yip. She remembered the timing because behind her, the phone had rung and she'd stepped in to glance down at call waiting. Her ex-husband, not in the habit of making frivolous calls. Jana gave a wave to her neighbors and picked up.

"Ronnie's dropping down for a visit," her ex said.

"That's nice," said Jana, but wondered why her son wasn't calling himself. "Do you think he'll stay over a night?"

"Yeah. I'm sure, yeah."

"Because I could get tickets for a show."

"Yeah, I'm sure he'd like that. Look, Jana, he wanted me to mention something before he got there."

Jana squeezed the receiver.

"He's dropping out of school."

"Well. I know he's been struggling. But I don't think he's giving it a proper chance, do you?"

"I know, I know," her ex said. "But he'll talk to you. He wanted you to have a heads-up, that's all."

"Of course. Well, he's put you in an awkward position, the bearer of bad news."

"It's okay. It's okay. Look, there's more."

"More?"

"But Ronnie will tell you."

Ronnie arrived that night, a Friday night. Jana had tickets for *Les Miserables*, Saturday matinee. They sat on stools in the kitchen nook, her with a glass of white wine, Ronnie with an underage beer. He thumbed the theater tickets. "Great seats." He slipped the tickets into their envelope and placed the envelope on the counter. "What happened—it's just, you know, I got there and it wasn't like high school. I couldn't deal with it."

Jana had discarded her first impulse, to lecture Ronnie on sticking it out, chin up, first semesters always tough, it would get better. She said, "Maybe you're right. Maybe a year off isn't a bad idea. What do they call it? A gap year?"

"It's more than a year," said Ronnie.

"Oh?"

"I'm going in the Army, mom."

"Now that," said Jana, "might be a bad idea." She gave a short laugh.
"It's a done deal. Off to basic next week."
Jana lifted her wine and wet her lips.
"It'll get my head straight, mom. It'll give me discipline. And there's the GI Bill coming out."
"Ronnie, your father and I can afford to give you an education." She tried a joke. "We don't need military intervention." Ronnie's eyes remained locked on his glass of beer, half gone, a thin head remaining. Jana said, "So this is okay with your father?"
"He's totally on board, mom. Says he wished he'd done it himself."
Her ex in the military? What a laugh. She hadn't been able to get him to walk around the block. She hadn't been able to get him to pick up his dirty clothes.
"They have specialties," said Jana. "Right? Which one did you sign up for?"
"Mom, if I'm going in, I'm going in as a straight-up infantry soldier."
"But, Ronnie, honey, look at you, you don't weigh a hundred and thirty. You can't stand the slightest pain."
Ronnie flushed. Wrong approach—stupid, stupid. She reached along the counter and took his hand. "Sorry, honey, you know me, just being a mom."
Saturday evening, after the show, after dinner, after Ronnie caught a Metro-North train up the east side of the Hudson, Jana dialed her ex. She assumed a neutral tone. "Wasn't there anything you could do to prevent this?"
"Jana, he has his own mind. You know as well as I—look, maybe this is good for him."
"Good for him? There's a war on. Boys are being killed."
"It's not that bad. Casualties are light. Hell, you're more likely to die here in an auto accident." Jana's head slumped. "You still there, Jana?"
"Yes. How's Elizabeth?"

"Oh, fine, you know, busy as always."
"And the kids?"
"Fine, fine."

Eight months later Jana caught a flight to Columbus, Georgia, the Metropolitan Airport, then the shuttle to Fort Benning. She listened to a speech on a stage in Infantry Hall by a one-star general and watched her son walk across for his ranger patch and a handshake. Outside, standing in the parking lot, Jana surveyed Ronnie and wondered how he'd done it. Dress pants bloused in paratrooper boots, airborne wings above his left pocket, ranger patch for his left shoulder, beret.

"A chip off the old block," her ex said.

"What do you mean?" said Jana.

"I mean you, with all your mountain climbing and outdoor adventures. He doesn't get it from me. Let's have a picture."

Ronnie extended an arm over her shoulder. Jana wrapped an arm around her son's waist. Her ex-husband snapped and two weeks later sent a five-by-eight proof. Jana and Ronnie stood leaning into each other, same height, same gray eyes, same full-lipped smiles.

• • • •

THE LAB TRIED TO SLIDE by on Jana's right. Jana planted a pole and stamped a boot. "Stay," she said. "Vamoose." The dog raised his eyes and consummated a tail wag. "Vamoose," Jana said. He folded his legs and lay in the trail with raised head and panting tongue.

"That will get you nowhere." Jana widened her eyes. "It's nothing personal."

Jana glanced at her watch, turned her head to the woods, and raised her voice, "Barry, I don't mean to be intrusive, but how's it going?"

His voice arrived from ten meters into the trees. "Need a few more minutes."

• • • •

TWO MONTHS AFTER RONNIE'S deployment to Iraq, Jana took a call from the garrison chaplain at West Point. Ninety minutes later he sat in Jana's kitchen nook with another officer, a captain, both in dress greens. The captain explained that they'd first notified her ex because that was her son's legal residence. They then drove downriver asking the ex not to call ahead.

"Of course, you must have had a premonition," said the chaplain. "But in a way it's better than us just showing up at the door."

Jana nodded. "Would you like some coffee?"

"Absolutely," said the chaplain.

They stayed for an hour.

In the days that followed, Jana received a letter from Ronnie's commander and emails from his buddies, and remembered she'd told the captain correspondence was okay. She pieced together the incident, a foot patrol through a village, with Ronnie, sensing something amiss, taking it upon himself to act as the team's rearguard. Militants appeared on the patrol's tail, gunning fast pickup trucks, firing RPGs and AK-47s. Ronnie's holding action saved the patrol.

The post-funeral reception was at the ex's, Ronnie's boyhood home, a spacious house with wide windows, sliding glass doors, and a view of the river. An eclectic mix. His high school chums, neighbors, work associates on both sides, relatives on both sides, plus the military. The reception had passed the solemn stage, had entered the chat stage with nods and laughs, aided by whiskey and wine.

Jana's ex stood among a circle of green uniforms. He extended an arm toward Jana and said, "Here's the one." She didn't know what he meant but felt obliged to walk over.

"Tell these guys," her ex said. "How many times have you climbed Breakneck Ridge?"

Faces craned in her direction.

"Breakneck," said one of the airborne rangers. "Wow."

Jana smiled. "It's not that difficult."

Her ex lifted his palms. "What did I tell you?" The soldiers laughed. "That's where Ronnie got it from. Not me." Her ex stared at his shoes. The light laughs from the soldiers trailed off.

A while later, Elizabeth took Jana in an extended embrace. "Oh Jana," she said, "this is so awful." True, thought Jana, but you have the second family. I only had Ronnie. Jana pushed the hard-hearted thoughts away, for Elizabeth had raised Ronnie from age ten, had been an admirable step-mom.

• • • •

THE LAB, FLAT ON HIS stomach, gave a low moan and wiped a paw over his snout. He raised his eyes to Jana.

"Mind yourself," she said.

Leaves crunched, twigs crackled, and Barry exited the woods. He leaned over and pushed his half-depleted baggie of toilet paper into the outer pocket of his pack.

Jana said, "Where's your carry-out?"

"My what?"

"Barry, you know the protocol. Leave no trace."

"Jana, I'm not carrying out a bag of shit."

"I realize it's distasteful—"

"Distasteful? There's no fucking way—"

Jana rapped Barry's pack with her pole. "You will kindly watch your language."

Barry's face reddened. "Jana, where do the animals go?" He pointed at the lab. "Where does this mutt go? There's shit all over the woods."

"You have," Jana said, "a tenuous argument for the feces, but not for the soiled paper."

Barry had closed his pack. He picked up his hiking poles and faced Jana. "It's covered up for God's sake. Nobody's ever going to see it unless they go searching."

"I'm very disappointed in this breach of etiquette, Barry."

"Etiquette my ass," said Barry, spraying spittle like a Shakespearean actor. "You want to carry it out? Come on." He motioned toward the woods. "I'll show you where it is."

Jana wondered if she, in Barry's place, would carry out a load of shit, or even soiled paper. The point being moot since she avoided such contingencies with an early coffee and the pre-hike movement it induced. She glanced at her watch.

"Okay, perhaps we're getting carried away."

"Yeah," said Barry, "I mean, I don't—"

"Let's forget it."

"Amen," said Barry. He shouldered his pack and cinched the hip belt. As he stepped off, the lab unbent its legs and rose. And this sad mutt, thought Jana, what harm can he do?

"Go on," she said with a wave. The lab lifted his eyebrows. "Go on," said Jana. "Permission granted."

A little lecture, Jana thought, this evening. She'd discuss it with Mike: people, for your own safety, do not pet or otherwise consort with domestic animals.

The lab caught up to Barry, went to pass on the left, but his snout caught a scent. He veered right and took two loud sniffs from the seat of Barry's convoy shorts, making contact on the second whiff. Barry thrust his groin forward, bent his knees, and twisted his head.

"Hey, watch it," he said.

The lab sidestepped left and barked. Oh, no, thought Jana, but the dog picked up its trot and disappeared around the next bend in the trail. A minute later, Barry disappeared. When Jana reached the bend, she stopped and took a long look to the rear.

All clear.

Wasteland

Snippets of Java code flitted between Doug's ears blocking the babble around Linda's work table: Georgia's high-pitched entreaties and propositions, Rama and Shawn's murmurs, Linda's interjections. Doug glanced at the time on his phone—almost the half hour, almost time for the meeting to end.

Linda's alto intruded, "Doug, do you have an opinion on this?"

He didn't but experience and sensitivity training told him one must be rendered. He nudged the bridge of his glasses. What was the point under discussion? Ah, yes, the calendar service needed a default sound for non-urgent notifications. Four sets of eyes engaged his.

"Something unobtrusive," he said.

The eyes remained engaged.

"But which gets the user's attention."

The eyes refused to let up.

"Like a tick." Doug tapped a fingernail on the table.

Nods and murmurs. Georgia pushed keys on her laptop. "Let's pencil that in. Okay, now I'd like to talk about the test schedule."

Linda put up a hand. "No. Enough for today." As Rama and Shawn escaped to the hallway, Doug unbent his knees and lifted his thin frame. Georgia gathered her laptop, twenty pages of printout, her notepad, phone, and two pens.

"Doug, I need you a minute," said Linda. She waited for Georgia's smile and exit before turning to Doug, her off-white blouse straining against its buttons. "How long do you need to code this thing?"

Doug lifted his eyes to Linda's face. "What level of effort?"

"Minimal."

"Six weeks. But—it won't meet Georgia's exacting standards."

Linda dropped into her chair and sighed. Doug followed her gaze to the upper right corner of the whiteboard on the far wall. Tomorrow was Friday, layoff day, not every Friday, fifteen weeks since the last, but always a Friday. Doug said, "Is there one coming?"

"That's what I hear from upstairs." From Danny D'Amato no doubt. Danny used to work with them in engineering.

"How bad?"

Linda swung toward Doug legs askew. Doug directed his vision to the whiteboard, wiped and ready for Linda's ancillary duty as grapevine central. On a layoff day, calls and emails filtered into her office and she posted the casualties in black markup. As official as company communication on the matter got. Employees below upper management would drift in and out to monitor the bloodletting.

"A dozen," Linda said. "More or less."

"Know who?"

"A few ideas."

Doug used to think he was immune with twenty-one years and a top-bracket pay grade. But he'd come to realize not only did he lack immunity but had entered the target zone, seniority these days more of a millstone than an asset. He wanted to ask where his head lay in relation to the chopping block, but knew Linda had said as much as she would.

Following a layoff, the company hired back, but at the low end, out of college or out of country, India and China favored. To avoid age discrimination lawsuits, layoffs crossed all demographics; but hiring back didn't. "I still say the money they save is not worth the dilution of talent."

Linda snorted. "We need talent? Look at what we're building."

Doug had no rejoinder. He thought about the meeting that had just ended. Their product: yet another calendar service with maybe one bell and two whistles not seen before. Not heavy stuff, not like the early years of meticulous research and serious development, their products today appendages of what already cluttered the marketplace.

"Anyhow," said Linda. She extended a hand toward the whiteboard. "Drop in tomorrow. If you hear anything yourself, you can contribute."

Oh, oh, thought Doug.

Linda peered and said, "What's the matter?"

"A scheduling issue. My father-in-law's in hospice."

"Sorry to hear that."

"If he dies tonight, I might have to take tomorrow off."

"Jesus, Doug, shouldn't you be there right now?"

"There's no point. He's unconscious."

Linda's wordless, outstretched lips clued Doug that he'd flunked another sensitivity test. But couldn't she, a product manager, understand the logic? That the man had passed from sentience, and there was no point visiting an inert body. And Doug had liked his father-in-law. A different style, blue collar, old-time union, worked in the GM plant his entire life, over-indulgent, overweight, but smart with cars. Many a weekend he and Doug had gone under the hood together.

Doug's thoughts returned to the scheduling issue. "What if somebody's getting laid off and they're not here on Friday?"

"You know, if my son ever tells me he wants to be an engineer, I'll slap him."

"Very funny, Linda."

"That's not a joke. As for your inquiry, they'll find you wherever you are and serve you."

• • • •

DOUG DROVE A TEN-YEAR-old Audi A4 in mint condition. He did his own maintenance. His father-in-law used to help. He drove the middle lane with cruise control set two miles over the limit and the sound system oscillating the mountain scene from an old rock opera. "I lift my eyes—to the splatter of rain." Drums and guitars, a riff of keyboard. "I spread my arms—to wind and pain."

Doug tapped the steering wheel and sang along. "Why doesn't the re-a-a-a-lity of life," boom, boom, "fe-e-e-el like the re-a-a-a-lity of life?"

This wasn't the soundtrack but a studio make-over. Danny D'Amato had seen the rock opera live in New York City and sneered at the studio version, but Doug liked it. Danny and Doug used to talk about such things in the old days when Danny worked downstairs. No more now that he had a perch with the vice-presidents and directors.

Doug dropped his right hand into his lap and gave a rub. He thought of the power of genital gratification, how it led men to lunacies like leering and wanking and worse, defying reason. He thought of the idiocy of wetting his pants over Linda, his colleague, unapproachable in the flesh. Then he thought of standing behind her, wrapping his arms, cupping his hands, pressing his phallus.

"Why doesn't the re-a-a-a-lity—"

Doug nosed the Audi alongside his wife's Toyota Highlander. The Highlander pointed out the driveway, and Mim stood by the driver's door. She said, "I'm going back to hospice. Eric's in his room."

Oh, oh, another scheduling conflict. On Tuesdays and Thursdays, Doug jogged after work. As he opened the car door, dropped his feet, and unbundled his body, his mind rummaged past couples counseling sessions for an empathic response that might segue to logical argument.

"Mim," he said, "I know how important it is for you to be there." Good start. He shifted weight to his left leg, then his right. "Eric should be okay alone for forty minutes. I mean, he's twelve."

Mim lifted her face to the sky. "Go for your run," she said. "I'll wait."

Doug raised his hands. "I mean—"

"Go. But could you get started, like, right now?"

Doug turned toward the house.

"Wait. One other thing."

Doug turned back toward Mim.

"You have to have a talk with Eric."

"Why's that?"

"Because it's disgusting what he's doing."

Doug's heart thumped.

Mim said, "Haven't you noticed? Biting and biting those fingernails. They're terrible."

Doug hastened through the front door, climbed stairs two at a time, and passed Eric's closed door. Fingernails. He continued to the master bedroom, undid shoes and socks, dropped his Dockers, dropped his Hanes. He slipped off his button-down casual and checked his profile in the full-length mirror on the inside of the bedroom door. Thin in the chest and shoulders with long legs but heavy thighs. Brown hair fading at the forehead, fading top rear. Horn-rimmed glasses with progressive lenses.

Downstairs, outside, Doug tightened his Adidas and lifted a left hand. "Thirty-five minutes."

Mim smiled. On this she could count, Doug knew. Thirty-five minutes meant two thousand one hundred seconds, no more, no less.

Doug dreamed of fleetness, of knees lifted, quadriceps parallel to the ground, feet bouncing on their balls, and forearms swinging in perfect synchronicity. But manifestation saw a stodgy, pigeon-toed ramble with forearms that flapped. Still, Doug managed seven-minute miles, better than most modern humans. Today he trotted his short circuit, his five-miler. He checked his watch at Fourth and Maple—a hundred and nineteen seconds, two seconds off. He adjusted his gait and felt better, felt on, felt the rhythm. "Oh, why doesn't the re-a-a-a-lity of life," he sang. At Fourth and Oak, Doug made a second time check. Spot on.

• • • •

NEXT MORNING, DOUG'S eyes opened at zero six thirty-nine. No Mim. He threw his legs from their bed and strode to the master toilet.

From the bedroom, an incoming text chimed. Doug finished his pee, washed his hands, and checked the message: dad still the same staying with mom. Doug summoned empathy and applied thumbs to keypad: tell mom am thinking of her.

Downstairs Doug popped a pod of breakfast blend in the Keurig and four Eggo buttermilk waffles in the toaster. Eric, a flounce of brown hanging over oval, black-rimmed glasses, slipped into the kitchen, took a stool at the bar, and said, "Is it true what they say about grandpa's dying, that it's before his time?"

"Yes," said Doug. "Six years and eight months."

"Why?"

"Smoking and excessive use of alcohol. And corpulence." The waffles jumped from the toaster. Eric leaned his forehead into his right hand.

Doug said, "It's okay, Eric. I know, it's sad."

Eric dropped his hand and lifted his head. "I was thinking of something else." His eyes engaged Doug's through their two sets of lenses. "Is it really impossible to square the circle?"

Doug hesitated. Coming of age, always ticklish. "It is."

"Why's that?"

"Because pi's transcendental." Doug finished spreading butter on the waffles and pushed a plate toward his son.

Eric said, "I'm really struggling with that concept."

"Orange juice or cranberry?"

"Orange. Half a glass."

Doug placed glasses of juice, a small jug of Canadian maple syrup, and his coffee on the counter. He took the stool next to Eric and said, "Okay, you understand pixels in digital imaging, right? Like little squares."

"Uh huh."

"But you can draw a circle with them? And it looks like a circle."

"As long as the resolution is good," said Eric. "Say twelve eighty by eight hundred."

"But if you magnify the screen or look at it in an icon editor, you see it's not perfect. It's jagged. Now suppose you keep increasing the resolution, can you ever make those jagged lines go away?"

"Okay, I see that. You'll never get to a perfect circle." Eric chewed on a piece of waffle and swallowed. "But why is it?"

"Because the pixels are still square no matter how small—"

"Right. I get the idea of the pixels getting smaller and smaller. It's like what Archimedes did inscribing polygons in circles."

"Good observation," said Doug. "So it sounds like you've got it."

"No, no, Dad. Why? Why is it we can't go all the way to a smooth circle? Why do numbers have to be transcendental? It doesn't fit in with—" Eric waved his fork. "—with the world."

"Ah. Semantics." Doug took a sip of coffee. He'd thought around this issue all his life, but how to squeeze it into a few pubescent words. "Okay, here's my take. We like to think what's in our head is real. But it's only what's in our head."

"But it's real inside our head," said Eric. "Right?"

Doug raised a finger. "If we see a tree, the tree in our head is not the tree itself."

"But it's the tree as we know it."

"Okay, let's try something else. Let's try numbers. We see five sticks. The sticks are real. We see five rocks. The rocks are real. But is the five real?"

"Well," said Eric, "you can do a lot with five without the sticks and rocks."

"You can. That's why it's insidious. It's so powerful what we can do in our heads, we think it's real."

"But it's not?"

"It's not. In my opinion. It just helps get us closer."

"That's kind of deep."

"You're young," said Doug. "You've got a lifetime to ponder it."

Doug moved the dishes to the sink and turned to his son. "There's something I've got to talk to you about."

Eric dropped off his stool. "Yeah, Dad."

Doug's eyes brushed Eric's nails. Gnawed to the quick.

"What is it?"

"Well, this summer, you want to do some hut-to-hut in the White Mountains, just the two of us?"

"You mean, like walking all day and sleeping in bunks?"

"Something like that. Fun."

"I'll think about it."

• • • •

NEXT DAY, DOUG AND Linda stood side by side inspecting her whiteboard. To Doug's left, at Linda's work table, sat Georgia. She chewed the left side of her lower lip and ran a hand through her hair. Her name appeared fourth on the list of ten.

Doug shifted his weight from left leg to right, and back. "This is so unfair," he said.

Georgia dropped her head in her arms. Linda brushed by Doug and put an arm over her shoulders. "Look, sweetie, you need references, anything I can help you with, just let me know. This isn't the end of the world."

Georgia lifted her head. She pulled her laptop and notebook and printouts toward her, her pens and phone. Linda kept a hand on her shoulder and the other on an arm, and guided her toward the door. She watched Georgia recede down the hall.

Doug said, "I guess that wasn't a surprise."

"No, I was pretty sure about Georgia." Linda looked at her phone. "It's going on two." She stared at the whiteboard. "They should all be in by now. But—you haven't heard any news?"

"Nothing."

"They need one more big head to get their money's worth."

Doug's phone buzzed. He stepped into the hallway and looked down. Not the company reaching out to his private phone; it was Mim. Doug swiped and put the phone to his ear.

"Dad passed," she said.

Doug had rehearsed this moment but didn't want it to sound rehearsed. He took a small breath and held it for a second before responding.

Linda's eyebrows rose as Doug stepped back into her office. "My father-in-law."

"Sorry," said Linda. "Why don't you get going? I'll let the others know."

"No rush," said Doug. "Mim will be home for Eric." He looked at Linda's outstretched lips. "The wake won't be till tomorrow."

"Doug, go home right now. Jesus Christ." Her desk phone buzzed. She picked up the handset and listened, replaced the handset, and walked to the whiteboard.

"Wow," said Doug as he watched the eleventh name take form. Danny D'Amato. Who would've thought?

• • • •

DOUG TIGHTENED AND knotted the laces of his Adidas and set off. His knees rose and the balls of his feet propelled him with the barest grazing of earth. His arms pumped in synchronous perfection, fists forward, elbows back, forward, back. He refused to glance at his watch for fear of jinxing the flow but sensed he was doing six—no, closer to five—five-minute miles, his strides exceeding two meters.

His course flowed uphill on a track of dirt and rock with solid wall on the right and sheer drop-off on the left, a Colorado jeep road, he realized. He'd been to the Colorado Rockies years before, and the roads to the trailheads could be as rough as the trails. Doug skimmed over rocks and potholes, ripples and washouts. His body experienced no strain; no burning lungs, no tearing calves, no drag on his gait. He was close to flying.

The wall on Doug's right receded to a slope. Ahead appeared a Buddha-like figure in light blue hospital bottoms, his naked belly flopping over the drawstring. He sat cross-legged amidst a pile of beer cans and cigarette packs. Smoke swirled from a filter-tipped ash in his left hand. His right hand tipped a pint of Southern Comfort. Doug sensed recognition and thought, no way, but when the pint came down, there it was, the cherubic face of his deceased father-in-law.

Doug raised his left palm. "Hi, Dad, how's it going?"

His father-in-law's mouth broadened. "Doug, my boy," he said, "good to see you. How's it going, you ask?" His arms opened like bat wings and his male mammilla jiggled. "Check it out."

Doug twisted his head to check it out, taking care to maintain stride. His father-in-law leaned forward, his stomach folds compressed like an accordion. "I love it here. I can do whatever the fuck I want."

Doug stuttered a step and stifled a gasp. In three years of dating and sixteen years of marriage, in all those years, not once had Doug heard his father-in-law drop the F bomb. Doug took a final glance over his shoulder. Wow. People really change when they're dead.

The road leveled and a copse of aspen appeared and in it a length of flesh. As Doug drew close, he saw that the flesh belonged to Linda in three-quarter profile, breasts sagging, nipples jutting. She turned full frontal with a Cheshire smile, her right hand behind her head, and her left hand entangled in the auburn below her tummy bulge.

Doug raised his left palm. "Hi, Linda. Nice pudenda."

"Thanks, Doug. You looking for a little get-off?"

Doug shook his head and laughed. "Not anymore. You see, I'm impervious to lust." Linda pushed out her lips. "It's true. Impervious."

Doug looked away and lengthened his stride. "O-o-o-oh," he sang, "why doesn't the re-a-a-a-lity of life," boom, boom, "fe-e-e-el like the re-a-a-a-lity of life?"

That's so true, thought Doug. Why didn't the accessible, like Mim and Eric, appear on these jaunts? Instead of the dead and the unapproachable? Where was this vaunted reality?

The sky blackened and rain slapped the trail. Doug inhaled its moisture but didn't suffer its stings. As if in a cocoon, he cantered cool and dry.

The rain dwindled and a left-leaning sun pushed bleached rays through lingering clouds. The jeep road had given way to a path of rough rock. Doug wasn't in Colorado anymore but closer to home, the White Mountains of New Hampshire, above tree line, on the Gulfside Trail. Doug recognized the pile of boulders called Mount Adams and knew in twenty minutes he'd be looking left into the abyss of King Ravine. But when the occasion arrived, his downward gaze met a phenomenon of fascination, no doubt resulting from the storm: a cloud inversion cloaked the ravine in frothy white from rim to rim. Above, azure skies. At Doug's feet, a roiling ocean of lather.

Doug wondered if he could jog upon the upper surface of low-lying clouds. So far, his fleet step had held him above the pits and protrusions of road and trail, so why not condensed vapor? On the next stride, Doug crossed right leg over left and yawed off the trail. He crossed again and lost half a meter of altitude. He crossed a third time and pressed upon heaven's halo.

He crossed again.

What About India?

At the start of the workday, Marsha felt fine. Perky, in fact, coffee pushed aside, eyes on her screen, fingers on the keyboard. She'd found a bug and posted a problem report—priority 2, in her opinion. A chat box from Randy, the project's senior development engineer, appeared.

hey marsha priority 3 not a functional problem

Yes, it was, she tapped back.

no marsha priority 3

Randy was one of the smartest people alive, but Marsha didn't buy not a functional problem. Maybe she'd go upstairs, meander the hallways and aisles, find his cube in the heart of brainland, and lay out the case for priority 2. But just then her supervisor's hand beckoned from a conference room where co-workers had been in and out all morning.

Marsha took a chair facing the supervisor, a friend, almost, same gender, a few years older. Words flowed from her mouth. Forms slid across the table. A packet appeared. More words flowed.

"Four weeks, with full use of the facility for those four weeks. That's very generous, Marsha. Severance pay, let's see, two weeks for every year, yes, twenty-four weeks. Not bad."

The supervisor raised her face, removed reading glasses, and told Marsha her performance was not at issue, that Marsha had fallen prey to market exigencies, had been caught in a major resource action with hundreds affected.

Marsha's stomach hurt. The supervisor slid a hand her way.

"Take the rest of the day off."

Marsha told her about the bug, how it should be priority 2.

"Marsha, go home. Take time for yourself. Oh. Next week. Set up a call with Rohit in the Bangalore office. He's taking your work."

Marsha powered down her cube, slid packet and laptop into her backpack, passed security, buzzed through glass doors, maneuvered by Jersey barriers, tramped black tar and white lines, and found her car, a Prius less than a year old with payments of four hundred a month. Had they needed a new car? It was a hybrid, good on gas, good for the environment. Her daughter Zoelle had taken the old car, a Corolla; she needed it for her part-time job at Barnes & Noble. Her husband Bill had a pickup, a Ranger from the last century. Three cars were borderline necessary, not excessive, but she might have looked for a good used car, cheap, paid cash.

Marsha thought about Zo, going into senior year, looking at colleges for the past three weeks, her heart pinned to a dorm room at Boston College. Zo resembled Bill, stringy, hawkish, not tall, not short. Marsha was shorter by a few inches. She'd acquired a slight tummy bulge, but nothing to fret over. Last visit her internist gave her an A—excellent labs, no lumps, sure, lose a few pounds, not a big deal.

Marsha thought about her mother-in-law—oh, how she's gonna love hearing about this. She lived with her boyfriend in an apartment over the garage of the boyfriend's sister's house. Her body had gone round, her hair stringy. She dyed it barn red. She worked at the Target next to the mall and thought Marsha's family thought her family was riffraff, beneath them. Not true. True that Marsha's upbringing comprised salaried jobs, home ownership, savings, and the accouterments of suburban white collar life. But her family didn't look down on wage earners, and Marsha didn't consider marrying Bill as marrying down.

Their neighborhood was Boston suburbia. The Prius passed scraggly woods and backyard fences. Off highway crouched shopping centers, strip malls, business parks, professional parks, real parks, and developments of coiling roads with their capes, ranches, splits, and colonials, their maples, oaks, and pines, their lawns and hedges. It was midsummer with its intense green, its drippy heat, above-ground pools, in-ground pools, sprinklers, droning mowers, the perfume of fresh-cut grass. Their house was a small colonial, circa sixties, on half an acre.

Marsha stopped at Market Basket for chicken legs, ziti, and marinara for a cacciatore. Also, a small flank steak for Bill, who tired of chicken and fish. And eggplant for Zo, who'd turned vegan two weeks ago. Cook the chicken separate from the sauce, not quite a cacciatore.

Marsha sat at the kitchen table, laid her head on her arms, and let her eyes water. Her stomach felt better. She pushed away and addressed the stove.

Zo arrived and skipped stairs to her room, responding to Marsha's callout with a text-me. Marsha brought her thumbs to her phone.

are you home for dinner

course what do you think zxxxooo

Marsha stirred the sauce, with forays to the living room window. A pickup stopped out front—not Bill's, but Bill's boss, Biff. The passenger door opened and Bill hopped out. A moment later, Marsha and Bill stood in the kitchen. They kissed.

"Where's the Ranger?" said Marsha.

"Fuel pump crapped out."

But Bill had a plan. Tomorrow, Saturday, he'd be helping Biff with some inside work, hanging cabinets. First, they'd pick up a pump and pop it in.

"Is Biff paying you for tomorrow?"

"You know what, they asked us over tomorrow night, after the cabinets, Biff and Fran."

Fran was Biff's wife. They had a sprawling ranch with a tiled patio and an in-ground pool. They'd be putting out barbecue, Bill said, beer, wine, just the four of them. Perfect weather and Fran was a hoot, right?

"So he's not paying you."

Bill leaned over the stove. What smelled so good? He lifted lids. Italian, his favorite. Was there an occasion?

"I do have an announcement."

Bill cocked his head.

"When we're all assembled."

Marsha lit a small candle. Diet coke for Zo, Chianti for Bill and her. She planned to announce before eating, but the moment passed. Bill never asked, intent on the cacciatore and flank steak. As the meal wound down and Zo cast her out-of-here look, Marsha rang a spoon on the side of her wine glass.

"Ta da."

Faces looked her way.

"Well, it was a rough day at work. I was let go."

Zo raised her eyebrows. Bill's mouth opened. Marsha explained the severance package, the twenty-four weeks. That they couldn't go on like before unless she came up with something, but jobs were scarce. They had to budget like that income was gone.

"Mom, what about BC?"

"Honey, we can talk about that later. Only. Well, think about UMass. It's a great school and you can commute."

Zo jumped from the table, face red, fists clenched, her life in ruins. How could her mother do this? She pivoted, ran upstairs, and slammed her bedroom door. Bill's head hung over his cacciatore remains. Marsha walked upstairs, knocked on Zo's door, talked to her through faux walnut, told her it was still early, she could apply for BC as well as UMass, see what she got in grants, look at the numbers, please. Marsha's phone buzzed.

ih8u ih8u ih8u zxxxooo

Downstairs, Marsha found Bill with the laptop. He could get the fuel pump cheaper online. Pop it in next week. Biff would give him rides meanwhile.

"Maybe we don't have to be that extreme."

"You said it yourself."

"We could get rid of the Prius."

"We'd lose on it. We have to keep those payments going."

• • • •

MARSHA SHOWERED AND slipped into a satin nightie, blue paisley, from Victoria's Secret. She sat on the edge of the queen, legs crossed, blanket and sheet turned down, ready for closeness and passion. After a few things were straightened out.

Bill exited the bathroom toweling himself, eyes running up Marsha's legs and nightie.

"Well, well."

"We have to talk," Marsha said.

Bill dropped the towel and sat alongside. He looped an arm over Marsha's shoulders. His other hand brushed her leg above the knee.

"You can't keep rolling over for Biff. We can't afford it."

Bill pressed his nose against Marsha's cheek.

"Are you listening to me? When's the last time you had a raise?"

Bill brought his face away from Marsha's.

"Look, Marsh, hon, let's not get into it now."

"When then? Tell me when. Tell me!"

"You know, Marsh, at least I have a job."

"Oh. I can't believe you said that. Throw it in my face."

Tears swelled.

Bill dropped to his knees, held Marsha about the waist with his head in her lap.

"I shouldn't have said that. I'm sorry. I'm stupid." Bill drummed the top of his head. "That's me, dumb as a stick."

Marsha took a few short breaths, a sniffle, a laugh.

The lights faded. Marsha's nightie departed. Kisses came, Marsha on her back, Bill on his side, leaning over. His fingers roused her left nipple. His lips moved to the nipple. Marsha felt calm, felt warm, felt Bill's hand tiptoe past her tummy, felt a beam of light as from a half-open door, heard a voice, soft, but not Bill's, her daughter's.

"Mom. Mom. Why aren't you answering my text?"

Marsha tilted her head to see Zo backlit in the doorway. Bill removed his lips from Marsha's nipple and tugged the sheet up.

Zo crossed to the bed and formed a seat against Marsha's left hip.

"Mom. I'm sorry for being such a bitch."

"Zo, don't say things like that."

"No, it's true. I told Sara, and my best friend tells me, she says how could you behave like a bitch when your mom's in crisis? Can I give you a hug?"

They hugged.

"You know, Mom, I can get you in at Barnes & Noble."

"Zo, you work at the Starbucks concession."

"I know everybody there. I'm in tight with the bookstore management. Like this."

"Thank you, honey. I'll take it under advisement."

• • • •

NEXT MORNING, BILL stood on the edge of the lawn, his carpenter belt draped over one shoulder, hammers hanging, Biff due in two minutes. He turned to Marsha.

"Sweetie, could you do me a teeny favor? Mom needs a ride to work."

"Did you tell her about the layoff?"

"She needs to be there by ten. Yeah. I mean, how could I not?"

Biff pulled up with a wave, Bill departed, and Marsha took the wheel of the Prius. Twenty minutes later, her mother-in-law opened the passenger door, displaying a face with a wide smile.

"Welcome to the riffraff, Marsh."

She turned sideways, got a leg and one buttock into the car, gave a push, and got the rest in. Pulled the seat belt and buckled up.

"Sorry. I couldn't resist that."

Marsha twisted toward her mother-in-law and turned her head to back out of the driveway. Her mother-in-law continued to prattle.

"Hope you're not offended. You know, you may not think so, but I was real happy about your office job. There in high-tech. I thought you guys had it made. Whoa, watch out for that Beemer."

Marsha swerved as the BMW to their front poked its nose through a stop sign. Her mother-in-law threw up a middle finger.

"Asshole. But then things started to happen. Heard it on the news. My sig-other says, he says, you know what, those jobs are going the same way the rest of them, right to the Pacific Rim. That's what he said."

Marsha stopped in the fire lane by the front entrance of Target. Her mother-in-law unbuckled.

"I can get you in here. You'd make team leader in two years."

She pushed the passenger door open.

"But first take the unemployment. Take it till it runs out, every nickel, the bastards."

She leaned over for her hug.

• • • •

THAT EVENING, BILL and Biff were attempting forward flips off the diving board. Eight o'clock, eighty degrees, poolside, Fran and Marsha in lounge chairs, whiff of fading barbecue, dimming sky, stars, cold white wine. Biff failed to complete a rotation and splashed on his backside. Fran jumped to her feet.

"Jesus H, knock it off, youse two. What do you do if you hurt your back, you stupid fucks?"

She sat down.

"Sorry about yelling at your hubby. The stupid fucks. A few beers and they're kids again. What's the matter? C'mon, what's the matter? Besides losing your job?"

"It's just ..."

"Yeah, yeah."

"It's just that Bill hasn't had a raise for years. Not making near union wages. No overtime. Things like that."

Fran drained her wine glass before replying, voice low. They paid Bill as much as they could. They gave him forty hours every week, week in, week out, never laid off even when it got slow. A bonus every Christmas. Most guys would suck cock for that. She poured more wine.

Marsha looked around. Four bedrooms and three-and-a-half baths on two acres of manicured lawn. Three-car garage, full basement. Shrubs, bushes, flowers. Small wood lots flanked the north and west edges of the property.

"It's just that it looks like you're doing okay."

"Let me tell you, this house, which Biff built with his own hands, is once again mortgaged to the hilt."

So they could buy a few lots, put up a few more houses, hope someone bought them, at a profit. Fran went on. They used to take two weeks off, take the kids to Disney every winter, didn't do that anymore. They used to eat out all the time. Now they ate in all the time. They used to go into Boston for Bruins games. Now they watched the Bruins on NESN.

Marsha sipped her wine. Fran sipped hers.

"I see the looks from our old friends from high school, like, you got money and we don't. But try running a business. What would you do if we didn't have the business?"

She jumped to her feet, wine sloshing.

"Stay off that fucking diving board, both of youse."

• • • •

MARSHA'S DAYS ON THE job wound down. There had been no formal announcement of a resource action, no list, but within departments, the marked ones were known. Chance hallway encounters induced eye aversion, a paling or reddening of the face, the half-smile nod, the gulp. Jokes—wished they were the ones getting out of there, getting a package.

Randy, the development engineer, one of the smartest people on the planet, got the ax too. Of course, he was in a different league—he would land on his feet. Google, Amazon, Apple, Meta, Oracle, Microsoft, dozens of companies Marsha had never heard of, start-ups. He would find a berth.

Meanwhile, he ranted. Marsha had meandered the upstairs maze, found his cube. Three other development engineers, all male, sat there, one in the spare chair, one on the edge of Randy's desk, the other cross-legged on the floor, chubby, bald on top, sides pulled into a pigtail. Randy, lanky with tangled dark hair, leaned back in his swivel chair, legs askew. He nodded for Marsha to join. She leaned against the entryway.

"Let me tell you, this place cares nothing about good engineering. Or good product. It's all profit. A bunch of bottom feeders. Shovel out shit and rake in money. You know why they're laying off? The real reason?"

Randy paused for a look-around.

"Because engineers in Bangalore and Beijing can be had at one-third our cost. Are they any good? Doesn't matter."

Earlier in the day, Randy had forced a meeting with Ben, the division manager, a vice-president. Randy knew Ben from younger days, from the polytechnic, both starting as engineers, Ben picking up an MBA and slipping away, climbing the ladder. Randy laced hands behind his head and reconstructed the meeting.

"So he starts off thanking me for my long and exceptional service, the layoff being no reflection on my abilities, forced by market exigencies, etcetera, etcetera. I say, 'Ben, for Chrissake, this is Randy here. Could we drop the bullshit?' 'Okay,' he says, 'look around. You know what they call a senior engineer? A needless expense. That's their thinking. They want cheap.'"

The cross-legged engineer interrupted.

"Yeah, they want us cheap. But not them. Not Ben, with his fat salary and stock options."

Randy stared at the ceiling.

"Not that fat. The real money's at corporate headquarters. The CEO. A few senior vice-presidents. Ben's a bit player."

Marsha wandered away, left the boys. It was hard to commiserate. Their salaries were in the hundreds of thousands. That did mean they had further to fall when jobs and prospects dried up. More of a splat.

• • • •

MARSHA ADJUSTED HER headset and dialed Rohit in Bangalore for the hand-off, eight in the morning, her time, eight in the evening his. Rohit spoke in that cadenced English where every sentence seemed to end with a question mark.

"I am so sorry to learn of your situation, Marsha."

"I'm sure you are."

Why did she have to say that? There came a pause.

"You know, Marsha, it is not so easy here."

Yes, jobs flowed in but the population was large and competition fierce. In high-tech regions like Bangalore, inflation overpowered pay checks. There was great stress. There was the feeling they could be spit out any time. Jobs were going to China instead of India.

"Listen, Rohit, I didn't mean to sound like that. I'm just upset."

"It is okay. I understand, Marsha, it is not your fault. Let me tell you what it is, it is the globalization of capitalism by the one percenters, just like the Hydra. Do you remember your Greek mythology? The Hydra, with many heads, devoured everything in its path and you could not stop it by cutting off its heads. Because two grew back for every one cut. It is the same now, but worse."

Rohit's words merged and faded. Marsha envisioned him in a martial pose, toes out, knees bent, planted in the center of the subcontinent, lopping off Hydra heads with a two-handed sword.

"Marsha, you have no control over your destiny."

"That's not true, Rohit. There's things I could've done."

Marsha paused. Rohit waited.

"I could've got on the automation team. But no, there I was plump and happy with my day-in, day-out, not learning anything. If I'd shown some initiative, if I'd looked around, if I'd got on automation."

Rohit interrupted.

"Marsha, Marsha, two people on automation got cut. It is not you. One day, they need twenty cogs. Next day, they only need fifteen. Kiss your ass goodbye."

Who got chopped in automation? How did she not know that? Rohit from the other side of the world was telling her what was happening in the next set of cubes. She wondered if he had a family? Did his wife work? Did they have money in the bank?

He was still talking about cogs.

· · · ·

THAT EVENING, AFTER dinner, Marsha and Bill sat at the kitchen table, Bill behind the laptop. Marsha's phone hummed.

fabnews zxxxooo

Steps sounded on the stairs. Zo appeared.

"You won't believe it. It's amazing. Guess. Sara. Sara's thinking of UMass too."

"UMass?"

"Yes, Mom, the University of Massachusetts."

Zo expounded. She could live at home, a big saving, not to mention the lower tuition, and UMass, what a great school. She'd commute with Sara, share expenses, use Sara's car most of the time.

"That's wonderful," said Marsha.

Zo floated back upstairs. Bill floated back behind the laptop. His eyes lifted.

"How's the job search going?"

"I've got some interviews lined up."

"That's great."

"That's not great. There's two hundred people looking at those same jobs."

"Something will come in. Just keep plugging away."

Marsha leaned over and glanced at the laptop screen. Power tools were streaming by. She raised the pitch of her voice.

"Yeah. Well, plug this."

Bill opened his arms.

"You know. This isn't easy for any of us."

But especially me, thought Marsha. You, she thought, you have your hammers, your nails, your Biff, your loud-mouth Fran, your Christmas bonus, your, oh where I am going with this? Where am I going?

· · · ·

MARSHA INTERVIEWED and lined up more interviews. She smiled, she talked, she demonstrated her proficiency. Supplied references. Was called back for second interviews. She expanded her search, took leads from headhunters, interviewed on Zoom with a start-up in Texas. They invited her down for a second interview.

"Houston?" said Bill.

"They're paying to fly me down."

Bill needn't have worried. The fly-down transmuted back to Zoom. A week later, the position had, in their words, no longer become available.

Bill's mom told Marsha to take unemployment and work under the table. A friend of her boyfriend needed help cleaning offices at night, twelve dollars an hour, cash. Twelve dollars under the table was like fifteen or more reported, good money.

In October, Marsha interviewed at Barnes & Noble, settling kitty-corner from the store manager at a small table. He looked up from Marsha's resume.

"You're way over-qualified."

Marsha smiled.

"Look, I like you, Marsha, I like your daughter. But I hire you, you're here a few months, then you pick up something in high-tech and, bam, you're gone."

"There's not a lot to pick up in high-tech. I could really use this job."

Next morning, the store manager called with an offer, as a bookseller. Money half Bill's instead of double, but health insurance, 401K matching, holidays, vacation days, sick days. Opportunities for advancement.

As Marsha fell into the job, one event remained painful, whenever a former co-worker walked in, like Jim, who used to work four cubes over. His face reddened as he stumbled through hi, good to see you, yeah, well, okay, gotta run. But the second time, not so bad. Third time, almost normal.

"Hey, Marsh, how's it going?"

"Hey, Jim. Okay. They still shipping those jobs to Bangalore?"

"Or somewhere. I heard they were closing shop in Bangalore."

"Really? Well, I hope you're safe."

"So far, so good."

• • • •

THREE MORNINGS BEFORE Christmas, Marsha opened her car door on the fringe of the parking lot, where the employees parked, and stepped into a northeast squall. Frigid fingers tightened her ski jacket hood and fled to her pockets. On the ground, leaves, dirt, and paper skittered; in the sky, clouds skipped against hazy sunlight. By late morning, Marsha had thawed. Felt comfortable amongst her books in the stacks. Bill buzzed with fabnews. Biff had delivered the Christmas bonus check.

Marsha couldn't hear the amount. Bill was hollering, and what were the sounds behind his voice? Marsha pressed the phone closer, heard traffic, heard banging, wind whistling, Biff yelling. He was coming up with another bundle.

"Are you working outdoors?"

"Oh. Yeah. Just tacking down a roof while we have the weather."

"Are you crazy? Does Fran know you're roofing?"

"Hon, I'm wearing my woolies. For God's sake, don't call Fran."

A few minutes later, Zo buzzed. Marsha stepped from the stacks and looked across to Starbucks. Zo's face flashed a come-hither.

"Mom, are you blocking Gram's calls? Please answer her, so she stops calling me."

Zo leaned over the counter and lowered her voice.

"She can get you some year-end inventory work."

Graveyard shift, over the table, but sixteen-seventy-five an hour, good money. Zo shifted eyes right and left.

"Do you want an espresso on the sly?"

"Can I get a biscotto with it?"

"I can't do that, Mom. It'll show up in inventory."

A little past dark, Marsha slumped in her car seat, hands in her jacket pockets, legs and shoulders shaking, waiting for the Prius interior to gain heat. Her head started planning dinner but wandered. Sure, they would make it, Bill and her, and Zo—they had assets, they had two jobs and Zo's part-time. Others were worse off. Rohit in India. But she felt dull. She felt discarded. Her phone buzzed in her right hand and she brought it out from her pocket. An unfamiliar number, local. She swiped.

"Hey, Marsha, it's Randy."

Randy? Marsha knew he'd landed at a start-up named ECBM. Maybe they needed someone. She straightened her posture.

"Marsha, you remember Ben? Our division manager? We're starting our own company, the two of us."

"Wow, isn't that risky? I mean, especially Ben, he's a vice-president where he is. He could be CEO some day."

Randy laughed.

"Not if the other vice-presidents have anything to say about it. Look, Marsha, we'll need a few people right away, in a month or so, as soon as the funding comes in. I thought of you."

"Yeah, well, I'm certainly available."

"Great, great."

The phone went silent. Marsha thought the connection had dropped. Then Randy's voice returned.

"It's not like what you had before. More like an office manager. And the salary, well, it's kind of commensurate with that."

"Nothing in engineering?"

"There's no engineering jobs."

"What? What are you guys building that you don't need engineering?"

"We need engineering. It'll be outsourced."

"All of it?"

"Well, maybe some component integration. Look, in-house engineering's no longer a viable paradigm."

"A what?"

"Marsha, our business plan wouldn't have a shot if it called for salaried engineers. Not when that work can be shipped to China."

"What about India?"

Jesus, did she say what about India? She imagined Randy's eyes narrowing, his lips extruding. His voice returned.

"Whatever. But right now China's cheaper. Look, are you interested?"

Marsha pulled her left hand from its pocket, unzipped the jacket halfway, and pushed down the hood. The Prius interior felt warm. Toasty, in fact.

There You Go

Everett flicks a toggle, and the chain circling the thirty-two-inch bar jolts to a stop. Blue exhaust clears in favor of the syrupy scent of fresh-cut pine, its amber-black pitch everywhere: the saw, his used-to-be-white T-shirt, his jeans, yellow work boots, yellow work gloves, inside his forearms. Everett rests the saw on the butt log of the prone pine. A brown-feathered sparrow lands on one of its sheared limbs and scolds the chopper with chirps and head bobs.

A quarter mile away, Donald's saw hums. It always hums. Everett swears that boy must saw one-handed, wielding axe and measuring stick with the other. He lugs in extra chains so as not to lose time sharpening. He lugs in a canthook to roll his logs away from the brush, ensuring they're fully limbed.

Everett doesn't hear old Warren's saw. Wonders why he still works in the woods.

Now he picks up the voice of Rachel Clarke, the boss's wife. She jabbers from the direction of the landing site a hundred yards off, hidden by thin pine. Everett imagines Harmon Clarke, head down, punctuating Rachel's oration with the occasional "ayup" or "if that be your thought." Rachel's droning stops and the woods crackle with the encroachment of foot falls. Everett has lit a cigarette but squeezes its flame with thumb and forefinger. He pulls on work gloves and heaves a branch to the other side of the stricken pine. He swings his double-edged ax, and another branch, jammed beneath the second log, pops free. As Harmon appears, Everett swings his ax into the stump of the cut pine, alongside his saw, and releases the handle. He wonders why the boss's lips are rippling in and out, their perturbed motion, and checks his tree. Straight, over two feet in diameter, four good logs, brush thrown over, or getting there—the boss should be happy.

Harmon stares at his work boots and says, "Afraid you're all done, Ev."

Everett turns his right ear to Harmon as though not having understood.

Harmon raises his eyes. "They ain't enough work going forward."

"Well," says Everett, "if it's a slack period, I can wait it out."

Harmon shakes his head. "It's worse than slack." He pushes the toe of his boot into sawdust and twigs. "When you come on, I told you then, this might be happening."

Everett wants to say, why not old Warren? But Warren doesn't take up two days' payroll a week, the piddling amount he chops. Everett wants to yammer about boy wonder, whose saw still hums, but can't think of substance for a complaint.

Harmon checks the state of his boots again. "Finish out the day," he says, "and tally what I owe you." He turns and fades.

• • • •

EVERETT'S PICKUP CLATTERS over Mill Stream Road, leaving a trail of dust. It turns into his dirt yard and its motor quits. Everett looks through the windshield at what started as a tarpaper shack and over the years acquired clapboards, molding, asbestos shingles, screened windows—stapled over with six-mil plastic come winter. There's a dug well with electric pump and expansion tank, and a dug cesspool for the kitchen sink and indoor toilet.

Everett pulls his chainsaw from the back of the pickup and stows it under a tarp by the front door. He makes another trip for ax, measuring stick, gas can, and files. Inside, his daughter Julianne sits at the kitchen table with the handset from the wall phone against her right ear, the cord dragged across the linoleum floor. "Yeah," she says. "Uh-huh. No I didn't. No, I never said that to nobody." She's fifteen.

On the stove, two pots simmer, one with peeled potatoes and a smaller with canned green beans. It's a twenty-inch gas stove fed from a propane tank outside the back door. Everett cracks the oven door and catches a whiff of burnt chicken leg from the top rack.

"Where's your ma?"

Julianne cradles the handset. "Hanging laundry."

Everett points to the stove. "You supposed to be watching this?"

"It's watching itself."

Everett grasps the phone cord, and the handset leaps from his daughter's hand. As he walks to the wall and slams the apparatus on the receiver, Julianne jumps to her feet and squeals like a raven. The back door opens and Everett's wife, Marion, pushes in with an armful of unfolded sheets. She says, "Now what?"

"I don't need no sass today," says Everett.

Marion drops the sheets onto the kitchen table. "Oh," she says, "is it sass you don't need?"

The rage starts in Everett's stomach, seethes to his shoulders, and contorts his mouth. He crooks right arm and hand above his head, palm open. Marion tries to step back, but her butt's against the table. Julianne puts both forearms in front of her face.

Everett's face sags and his hand drops to his side. "Go on," he says, "I'm not a'hitting anyone." Julianne runs from the kitchen.

Marion slides along the table and steps back. Her voice eases. "What happened?"

Everett twists his body a quarter to the left. "I got let go."

"Well," says Marion. She takes a step toward Everett. "We knowed that situation weren't stable."

"The wife," says Everett. "Rachel. She come out to the job. I hear them a'talking. Then he comes popping through the pine and tells me. Don't even look me in the eye."

"I don't doubt but she checked their books and you don't fit there no more. You going back with Williams, then? If he'll have you."

"What else?"

"She was always good with books, that Rachel." Marion bends and opens the oven, which emits a thunder cloud. "God damn that girl. Can't do one simple thing."

Everett says, "What about you? Your job be holding up?"

Marion turns off the oven and straightens. "Oh, you bet. It'll be there just afore hell freezes over."

• • • •

EVERETT CLASPS HANDS in front of his belt buckle, interlacing his fingers. He wears polished green work clothes, shirt and pants. He's shaved and put a part in his hair and stands next to Williams outside the doorway to the office of Williams Woodworks. The office, housing Williams and his clerk, hangs off a hallway running from an exterior door to the shop floor. Williams says, "So maybe you ought not have left in the first place."

Everett lifts his eyes.

Williams says, "Give up steady work for that big money in the woods."

Everett lowers his gaze to the wide hemlock boards of the hallway floor. They've been painted dark brown the past year, swept and mopped the night before.

Williams says, "Now you know how it goes, don't you?"

"Yessir, Mr. Williams."

Above the whining and banging from the shop floor comes a scream followed by a loud and elongated "shee-it." The shop foreman saunters into the hall with a head motion back toward the floor. "Little Al," he says. "Jammed his thumb in the press."

"Bad?"

"It ain't pretty."

Everett tries to put the thought away: if Albert can't work, they're down a man. He raises his face and looks into the close-set eyes of the foreman. They never got on well, Everett and the foreman, less so after Everett gave his notice. The foreman turns and Williams follows him to the shop.

Everett stands alone in the hall breathing wafts of cut wood, sawdust, and glue. The whines and bangs have resumed. A few minutes later, Williams returns with his foreman, muttering, "A floor full of morons, I swear."

The foreman shakes his head.

Williams says, "Put him to sweeping and cleaning. Make sure he keeps that gauze on."

"You bet, Mr. Williams." The foreman's eyes fall on Everett a last time before turning to the shop floor.

Williams says, "Well, Ev, I'd like to help you." His head flicks toward the outside door at the other end of the hallway. "But we're full up."

• • • •

NEXT MORNING, EVERETT follows a stubby man into a square enclosure formed from five-foot-high metal partitions and sits in a straight chair alongside a gray desk. The man waddles when he walks and wears a white shirt and necktie. He has a round face, scrubbed, with round, gold-framed glasses. His fingernails are clipped and clean. His teeth are perfect, not false perfect but real teeth taken care of.

Everett squirms and views the dirt-encrusted hands in his lap.

The man with the gold eyeglasses says call him Tim, mind if he calls Everett by his first name? His voice puts on back-country, but he's town through and through. Everett nods. Tim glances at Everett's filled-out forms on the desk. "Been looking much?"

"Nossir. Was hoping you could help in that regard."

Tim sits back. "Is woodworking all you know? That and chopping?"

"Yessir. That's all I ever done."

"Well." Tim taps a pen on his desk. "It's a handicap these days, don't you know? If you'd done metal. But even there, jobs are getting scarce."

Everett looks back to his hands.

Tim swings in his chair so he's in profile to Everett. He swings back. "Tell you what. But you got to promise me. You won't reject it out of hand."

Everett nods at his hands.

"There's a position come open at the Grub 'n Go."

Everett's face warms. The employees at Grub 'n Go wear striped shirts and paper hats, in public, seen by everyone. They say things like, can I take your order please? Do you want extra sauce with that? The ones out back flip burgers. The ones out front clean tables and empty trash.

"It's full time," says Tim, "and they're a'looking for a real a-dult." Pronounced with a long "a," as though he lived out on the dirt roads.

"I never done anything like that," says Everett.

"They'll train you." Tim leans over the desk like he's letting Everett in on the secret of creation. "It may not seem much first glance, but the pay's near what you've ever had. And—" Tim presses closer. "You get days off and health insurance."

Everett says, "My wife gets us health insurance already."

"That's good, but you never know. And there's a four-oh-one retirement plan."

Everett remembers the last time he was at Grub 'n Go. The woman ahead said, I don't want no pickle on my burger. And the woman behind the counter said, no ma'am, you don't have to have no pickle. We'll special order that burger.

"It's indoor work," says Tim. "It don't break your back." Tim lifts the receiver from his beige desk phone and pecks at the phone's keypad. He leans back, listens, then says, "Sue, how are you these days? Tim here at unemployment."

Everett pictures himself special-fixing a burger. No pickle.

"It's a man," Tim is saying. Everett's ears consume smatterings of female voice. Tim says, "Have I ever steered you wrong?" More chatter from the other end. Tim says, "You bet."

He hangs up and smiles. "Tuesday morning. Ten o'clock. Get there a few minutes early."

Everett doesn't return the smile.

"You don't need to interview or nothing," says Tim. "They're taking you on probation."

The shame rises and reddens Everett's face. A child's job.

"Everett." Tim's eyes float oversize behind his gold glasses. "The work you used to do is gone, or going that way. Now, you get over there Tuesday morning and give it a try." Tim sighs. "Okay, You're thinking, what if it don't work out, what if I hate it. Your unemployment money will still be here. Don't be worrying about that."

• • • •

LATE AFTERNOON, EVERETT sits at the kitchen table. Marion walks in and says, "Well?"

"They want me to work at Grub 'n Go."

"Do they?" Marion places a brown bag of groceries on the wooden counter top and opens the refrigerator. She turns her head. "Where's Julianne?"

"She got an after-school activity."

Marion drags a quart of milk from the bag and pushes it onto the top shelf of the refrigerator. "And what be that? Does it have anything to do with the Dolan boy?" She pulls a package of pork chops from the bag.

Everett slaps the palm of his hand on the table top. His voice lifts. "I'll tell you this, Mr. Man, you won't find me working for no Grub 'n Go."

Marion drops the pork chops on the counter and turns to Everett. "What are you doing instead?" She turns back to the refrigerator and stows the pork chops. She talks with her bent back toward Everett. "Are you taking their unemployment then? How long will that last?"

Everett hears the squeak of worn brakes and the sputter of a car motor, and looks out the front window. "It's the Dolan boy, all right." Marion closes the refrigerator door and approaches the window. "Oh, that girl, she's asking for a strangling."

• • • •

RACHEL CLARKE TOPS the list of people Everett could do without seeing, but here she comes, high-stepping into Grub 'n Go, trailed by her daughter, same age as Julianne. Rachel wears a straight skirt and button-down blouse. She boasts mega breasts, but not the enticing kind, the get-out-of-my-way variation. A beehive bouffant complements her stature and attire. The daughter wears a plaid, pleated skirt and white blouse, uniform for the nearby academy. She's been to Everett's house twice, for Julianne's ninth and tenth birthday parties.

A month has passed and Everett's off probation, working the counter, wearing a practiced smile. Rachel stops, steps back, steps forward, then postures with hands on hips. "Well, I do believe, don't you look official in that smock and hat. And I never seen your fingernails clean afore." Rachel elbows her daughter's arm. "Say hello to Mr. Evans."

"Hello, Mr. Evans."

"Hello, Trish." Everett deploys his chit-chat. "You been keeping up with them studies then?"

"Yessir."

Rachel glances over her shoulder. "Well, I best order. You got yourself a line."

Rachel and Trish chew their burgers and fries. Everett takes orders from the queue of after-school customers. As Trish slurps the last of her Coke, Rachel approaches the counter, which has cleared of customers.

"We had to let old Warren go," she says.

"So I heared," says Everett.

"And we don't have hardly enough to keep Donald busy these days. Not like it used to be." Rachel shakes her beehive. "Them landowners. Don't you know, they want top dollar for their lots, but when you cruise them, there ain't nothing there but scrub and knots."

"It's a shame," says Everett.

Rachel says, "So this is full time, this job?"

"'Tis."

"You got yourself a good situation, Everett." Rachel looks about. There's no customers waiting, but her daughter stands at the door shifting from one shoe to the other. Rachel turns back to Everett. "And Marion, she's still employed, right?"

"Sure enough."

"It's a state job she's got, isn't it?"

"Not exactly. The place she works for contracts to the state." Rachel waits for more. "They do the rest areas. Cleaning toilets, taking away the trash."

"Steady then?"

"Yes'm, forty a week."

"Well," says Rachel. She lifts her shoulders and chin and gives Everett a nod. "There you go, two good paychecks. With a little frugality, you're set. You're—"

An old-timer, ruffled gray hair and calloused hands jutting from a pea-green wool shirt, stands alongside Rachel. He nods to her and turns his attention to Everett. "I could do with another ketchup."

"By gawd," says Everett, "you can have two or three if you want."

The man's stubbled face crinkles. "By gawd, I'll take two then." He closes a hand around the packets pushed across the counter, nods again to Rachel, and turns back to the chairs and tables.

"You're not a drinker?" says Rachel.

Everett peers at a knick in the counter and passes a thumb over it. "Some," he says.

Rachel lifts a forefinger. "Give it up. Besides the trouble, it's wasted money."

Now Rachel examines the backs of Everett's hands, which rest on the counter. "And smoking too," she says. Over her shoulder, Everett watches Trish leaning against the door jamb with one shoe raised, its heel scratching the inside of her other stocking. Her lips are parted, and Everett notices turquoise braces on her upper teeth.

"Wasted money," says Rachel. "Harmon, he don't drink and he don't smoke."

"Yes'm."

Rachel turns to the door. She turns back and presses against the counter.

"It warms my heart to see you doing well, Everett."

• • • •

THAT NIGHT, EVERETT says, "Seen Rachel Clarke today."

Marion looks up from a half-knit sweater. "Did you then?"

"Said she was glad to see us getting on so well."

"Ain't she the sweet one." Marion works another stitch. "What you doing about fixing the truck?"

"Old Warren has a junk out back. I can have the alternator for the taking."

"You give him something, even if it's ten dollars."

"Sure."

"What you doing about our plumbing? That can't be freezing again come January."

Everett stands. "I guess I'll go out for a smoke."

"I guess you will."

Everett crosses the rear threshold and closes the door behind him. He scans the night sky for Polaris. Pretty sure he's found it. Heat tape and insulation, he thinks. Forty feet should do it.

Hippasus of Metapontum

The ship's ladder swayed left and right, along with the contents of my stomach, forcing a frantic clamber from the center hold with no time to admire the hazy half-moon over the bow. I grasped the port-side rail as we surged uphill at the incline of a three-four-five triangle, teetered on wave's crest, and plummeted at the same pitch. Except for last night's supper, which rose and spewed over the rail into the white-capped brine.

"Aye," said a voice beside me. "Let her all out. You'll feel the better for it."

Out it gushed, mutton and wine, followed by a dry retch. I pulled the sleeve of my tunic across my mouth and looked to the source of the nocturnal wisdom, a wide face of white stubble beneath a bald pate. His frame resembled a barrel set on two staves. He wore nothing but a sleeveless, white chiton against the night draft, and stood upon the galloping deck as I would Mother Earth on a calm afternoon.

"My advice, sir," he said, "take some air before retiring. It'll settle ye stomach and steady ye legs."

The ship fluttered on another crest, and my fingernails cleaved the rail as we dove for the wave's trough. My companion smiled, planted to the deck as steady as the mast behind him.

"And I would welcome a chat," he said, "to break the monotony of the watch."

"If you please," I said, "who am I addressing?"

"Orestes the mariner ye are, my young sir, sometimes called Orestes the ancient mariner."

"What's your age, then, ancient one?"

"Not a clue, sir, but I've been asea longer than anyone I know, including Kastor, the master of this boat."

My stomach calmed, as did the ship, not soaring and diving as before. Or perhaps my imagination and sickness had exaggerated the turbulence. I removed one hand from the rail and straightened my posture.

"Now, good sir," said Orestes, "tell me, what is this distinguished group we convey to Miletus? Are ye mathematicians?"

"We're mathematicians and philosophers," I said. Then added sotto voce, "Followers of Him."

"Ah," said the ancient mariner, "Pythagoreans."

"Indeed," I said, surprised that a simple sailor possessed knowledge beyond the myths of the sea. "We're on our way to a conference."

"And which of your greybeards is the illustrious Philolaus? He must be the oldest and loudest, the one with the curly-haired lad in tow."

Again, a surprise. That an ordinary seaman knew the name of a philosopher, albeit one of renown. However, he'd erred regarding identity.

"No," I said, "that's not Philolaus. The one with the lad is Hippasus."

"Of course," said Orestes. "I've heard of him, too. A contemporary of the great man, of Him himself, am I right?"

"You're correct." What an extraordinary fellow, I thought—knowledgeable, inquisitive....

"And the lad?" said Orestes.

"The lad is Demetrios, assistant and ward to Hippasus."

Orestes clapped his hands. "Aye, we should all have the assistance of such ruddy cheeks." He extended an elbow as if to nudge me. "And I don't mean the ones upon his face." I indulged his coarse humor with a chuckle.

"If it's Philolaus you're looking for," I said, "think of the most reserved, the sternest person aboard."

"Ah, I know the one you mean. Who can miss him?"

"He represents the predominant view despite Hippasus's seniority."

"Do they get along," said Orestes, "Hippasus and Philolaus?"

I moved my face close to the mariner's toothless countenance. "Not at all," I said. "Philolaus considers Hippasus a heretic."

Orestes raised an eyebrow. "How so?"

"Hippasus doubts the harmonics of numbers. He says there exist numbers that are not true ratios."

Orestes rubbed his chin as though considering the suggested abstraction. "Aye, but suppose there are such numbers?"

I took a half step back releasing my grip on the rail and losing my balance. Orestes threw out a forearm which I clutched.

"No disrespect meant, sir. I'm just saying—is there any way to decide the issue?"

Again I leaned into the sailor's sagging face. "Tomorrow at noon Hippasus is making a presentation. We're putting up a sandbox amidship, weather permitting."

"It should be a fine day, sir. This bit of roughness will pass."

• • • •

NEXT DAY, ON A CALM sea, as Helios's chariot approached its zenith, Demetrios, wearing a light blue citron with gold trim, and no undergarments, raked the sandbox smooth. A semicircle of thirty Pythagoreans watched, Philolaus at one edge, arms crossed, Hippasus in the center. My perch lay midway in the second rank, where I craned my neck, edged out by the greybeards. I felt an elbow in my left rib cage and glanced to my side to see Orestes.

"You take an interest in mathematics?" I said.

"Aye, sir, and astronomy. It keeps us afloat."

Hippasus stepped forward, turned, and faced us, a tall body with angular face and slanted smile, contemporary of the great man, Him himself. "We seek the truth," he said. "Do we not?"

I looked to Philolaus for a hint of reaction, but he was wont to give emotive displays.

"Yes, yes," said the Pythagoreans, "get on with it."

Hippasus turned to Demetrios and said, "Would you be so kind as to draw two lines, one perpendicular upon the other?"

The boy placed a stick with a cord in the sand, stretched the cord, and snapped it to create a line. He attached a second stick, drew arcs, aligned the cord on their vertices, and snapped a perpendicular.

"Well done," said Hippasus. "Now mark off ten equal measures on each line."

Demetrios shortened the length of cord between the two sticks and bent to the task.

"A fine lad," whispered Orestes.

"Now," said Hippasus, "connect the ends to form a triangle."

I bent sideways toward Orestes. "Are you following this?"

"Aye, sir, he's making a right isosceles triangle with the legs measuring ten units each."

Hippasus raised a finger and his voice. "Do we agree that the area of each leg of this triangle comprises a hundred squares? And that the hypotenuse—" Hippasus pointed to the last line snapped by Demetrios. "And that therefore the hypotenuse is the root of two hundred squares."

"Yes, yes," said the greybeards.

"But what is the precise value?" said Hippasus. "Demetrios, mark off the hypotenuse using the same measure as for the legs."

Swinging the two sticks, Demetrios marked fourteen measures along the hypotenuse, the last falling just short of the end. The boy swung again and the fifteenth mark fell beyond the end of the hypotenuse. A murmur swept along the semicircle, more of dismay than surprise, for the problem was known, if not the solution.

"Clearly," said Hippasus, "the hypotenuse cannot be apportioned in terms of the legs."

"Come, come," said a greybeard. "You just haven't found the measure."

"I've tried every number to ninety-six, with great care, on large plots of sand. Nothing comes out. As the measure grows smaller, the line approaches a harmonic. But it's obvious that it will never get there." Hippasus pointed into the sandbox. "The hypotenuse of this triangle is immeasurable."

"Impossible," said a greybeard.

"Absurd," said another.

Philolaus unfolded his arms and stepped into the sandbox. He lacked the height of Hippasus and his sonorous delivery, but eyes of coal shriveled the strongest heart. He ground a sandal in the center of the hypotenuse, looked first at Hippasus, then the rest of us.

"This is not a proof," he said.

"Of course it's not a proof," said Hippasus. "It's a demonstration so even the most dense among us can understand the issue. Even that bowlegged gaffer."

For an instant, I thought Hippasus was pointing at me, my loins puckering until I realized he meant Orestes, who said, "Aye, sir, and I take your meaning."

Laughter rippled from the Pythagoreans except for Philolaus.

"There is a proof," said Hippasus. "A proof by contradiction which I intend to present at the conference." He cast a finger at the trodden hypotenuse. "I will show beyond doubt that this line is immeasurable."

A gasp arose, more for the tone of Hippasus's remarks than their substance. Although the substance was, in fact, the problem.

"Your so-called proof is not on the syllabus," said Philolaus.

"What are you afraid of?" said Hippasus.

・・・・

NIGHT PASSED WITHOUT incident, neither the sea nor my stomach churning. I was making a breakfast of flatbread, goat cheese, and grapes when yells and thumps assailed the center hold from the adjacent greybeards' cabin. A scream, the voice of Hippasus, then muffled echoes.

We looked around, us lesser philosophers, but made no move. It was not for us to dispute the actions of our begetters. We heard grunts rising toward the deck and took our own ladder into a post-dawn mist on an undulating deck. Eight greybeards stood about a squirming mass the length and breadth of Hippasus, wrapped in two cloaks, tied with cord top, middle, and bottom. There must have been a rag stuffed in his mouth for he emitted only inarticulate gobbles.

Two greybeards swayed across the deck and staggered back under the weight of a bag of sand gripped between them. They plopped it midway on the squirming sack of Hippasus and secured it with another cord.

I backed away from the proceedings and saw Orestes standing amidst his shipmates. He walked my way. I said, "They're just trying to scare him."

"I fear you're wrong, sir. They mean to drown him."

I edged closer to ensure our privacy. "But he had a mock court if any. These actions are akin to murder."

"Not," said Orestes, "if the master of the boat agrees."

I looked to the helm where Kastor stood, legs apart, arms crossed, thick black hair rippling in the wind, eyes above the fray.

"How could he agree to such an extremity?" I said.

"Scuttlebutt has it he's been promised the curly-haired lad for the duration of the voyage."

I looked to Orestes for a sign of disgust or distress, but his demeanor appeared whimsical as he gazed west. I looked again to the master of the ship, then back to the commotion upon the deck. The greybeards, four to a side, were dragging Hippasus to the port-side rail.

I said to Orestes, "Did you understand the demonstration yesterday? The immeasurability of the hypotenuse?"

"Aye."

"Doesn't he make sense? Isn't he on to the truth?"

At the port-side rail, sixteen hands grasped and lifted.

"Heave," said Philolaus.

The wriggling cloaks, corded and sandbagged, held the sea's surface for a pulse beat then sank. For a second pulse beat, the sack remained visible in the blue-green Aegean then faded beneath the ripples. Philolaus and the greybeards turned and marched away as having disposed of a dog gone mad.

"Aye, the truth," said Orestes.

Of a sudden, the deck surged from port to starboard, and back. Whitecaps appeared on cresting waves.

"Poseidon is angry," I said.

"Nonsense, sir," said Orestes. "Ye don't believe those fairy tales, do ye?" He pointed west. "This storm's been in the making since afore dawn. But look at ye, sir."

I stared into Orestes's countenance to catch his meaning as wind and sea roiled the ship under scattered droplets. The deck had cleared except for Kastor and a handful of mariners trimming the sails.

"Why you're rooted to the deck as if born asea, sir. You're a natural ye are, once you got by the puking."

I flushed with pride at my newfound mariner's legs but the next roll of the deck sent me skittering sideways.

Orestes gave a short laugh. "Nevertheless, sir, ye best get below."

Aye, below.

Negative Entropy

Professor Gladstone's age? Cindy had guessed fifties with his steel hair and bushy eyebrows, but at close range, surveying a face of furrows, upped the estimate to mid-sixties. He sat behind a beige metal desk with a faux oak top and beckoned with his left hand. Cindy, briefcase clasped to her chest, positioned her rear on the edge of the office's twill sofa. Earlier, Cindy had asked Theresa, the only other female doctoral candidate, about Gladstone. Theresa had laughed and said, just make sure he keeps his pants on.

Gladstone removed reading glasses, reducing his brown eyes to normal size. He lifted the thin sheaf of papers on his desk and dropped them. "This won't fly, Cindy. You don't mind if I call you Cindy?" He sat back. "But don't worry, we'll hammer out a viable proposal. I have a few suggestions."

Cindy smiled and said, "You disagree that entropy is connected to time?"

"I do disagree that it can be reversed at the macro level to produce a time machine." Gladstone leaned forward. "We'd be laughed out of the department."

"Would we, Professor Gladstone? Because I've fabricated a prototype." Cindy tapped the left side of her jaw. "An implant that lets me drop back twenty seconds and adjust what's already, allegedly, occurred."

"Absurd."

"I know, for example, that you're not wearing your pants, that you're about to stand and expose your genitals, because you've already done it."

"What?"

"But I can alter our timeline. I can protect myself. Do you know how?"

As Gladstone remained rooted to his chair, mouth agape, Cindy dropped her right hand into her briefcase, and extracted a black cylinder topped by nozzle and trigger.

"With Frontiersman Bear Spray," she said rising and popping the safety tab.

Gladstone threw up his forearms, a futile gesture, as Cindy pulled the bear spray trigger and applied a three-second blast. Her thesis advisor tumbled sideways under a gray cloud tinged with orange. Cindy circled the desk planning to grasp Gladstone's testicles until he passed out. But the senior citizen writhing on the floor wore tan Dockers from waist to ankles, belt cinched, fly zipped.

"Oh my god," said Cindy. "I'm so sorry, Professor Gladstone."

Gladstone lifted himself to a sitting position, tears streaming over his cheeks.

"I don't understand," said Cindy. "I know what I saw in the future. And probability allows for negative entropy—"

"At the micro level," said Gladstone. "An atom here, a molecule there." He coughed and slavered. "At the macro level, it's impossible."

"Oh I'm so embarrassed, my bad."

Gladstone held out his hands. "Help me up."

Cindy tugged. Gladstone teetered to his feet and gained his chair. Cindy retreated to the couch and sat on its edge, knees together, briefcase clutched in her arms.

Gladstone looked up from Cindy's thesis proposal and removed his glasses. Cindy didn't see a hint of anger or distress in his face. His eyes appeared clear and dry. He said, "I simply can't allow you to go forward with this proposal. It's been beaten to death at the micro level and has no credibility at the macro level."

Cindy sniffed the office air but couldn't detect a whiff of pepper. Her right hand dropped into her briefcase and fondled the canister of bear spray. The safety tab was still in place.

"I've scribbled down a few ideas," said Gladstone. "I'll come around and show you."

His chair scraped back, and he rose.

Cindy screamed.

Mind Over Matter

Maisie stood on the kitchen deck watching the pickup accelerate to the end of the driveway and swing right. No brake lights, the two in profile: little Carl on the near side, big Carl behind the wheel. Little Carl came to his father's shoulder so Maisie could see both heads of black hair, both noses frontward like hawks after field mice. Maisie knew Carl's driving habits: he liked to go into curves fast, not switching pedals until the last second.

The morning was early spring—fifty degrees, no clouds, sun touching the treetops across the road, snow gone except for patches in the woods, hardwoods budding. Black flies not out yet. Nice time of year in the north country. Maisie was short, five-two, with small breasts and behind, resembling Ma. Years ago, Maisie had dirty blonde hair; now it was streaked gray, while Ma's was fully blonde.

As for the pickup, any fool could see the front left brake cylinder leaked, could see the stains on the wheel, smell the acidity, say *better get that fixed*. Instead, Carl bought brake fluid by the quart at Walmart and topped off the reservoir each morning, leading to the first theory of causality—that the wheel cylinder failed catastrophically when Carl jammed the brakes at the last second. The deficiency in that theory was that the other wheels should have caught if only for a second, but no skid marks were evident.

The second theory of causality also had a deficiency, but the police chief resolved it with logic and her knowledge of behavioral science. Two days after the funeral service, she presented herself in Maisie's driveway, a short stretch of tar running up to and alongside the deck, ending at an eight-by-twelve-foot tin shed.

The boys from the state police lab had examined the accident scene and the truck, the chief told Maisie. The chief was middle-aged, mid-sized with dark hair and a round face. Her bust strained the buttons of her uniform shirt, giving a matronly, rather than a sexy appearance. She had a few questions, but, she said, Maisie didn't have to talk to the police if she didn't want to.

"It's alright," Maisie said.

Well then, did she know about the problem with her husband's truck?

"Sure enough," Maisie said.

She led the chief past her worn Honda Civic to the shed. Its door hung open on a broken hinge. Inside were metal shelves.

"Right there," Maisie said.

The chief reached in and hefted a quart of brake fluid.

"I got to tell you, there's one thing really bothering me," she said. The lab had found the brake reservoir empty. But the school bus driver had said the hood was up on the truck when she stopped. That was a half hour before the accident. What was he doing with the hood up if not attending to the brake fluid?

No response.

The chief said, "Could you walk me through what happened that morning?"

Maisie assembled the events in her head. After breakfast, Carl was bent under the raised hood of the pickup. Beside him was a container of brake fluid. Beyond, the school bus stood until Carl looked up and waved off the driver. Maisie went to little Carl's bedroom and pulled up an earphone.

"You just missed the school bus."

"Don't sass me, woman," said little Carl, pushing her hand away. "Pa will drive me."

"Well, here he comes," said Maisie, and little Carl jumped up.

As little Carl ran to the kitchen, big Carl said, "Get back with your game. I have to take a shit."

To Maisie, he said, "Make yourself useful, woman, and put that brake fluid back in the shed."

These were Maisie's thoughts. For the chief, she summarized.

"Well, he was in the driveway. I heard the school bus. Then he come running in for the bathroom. He was in there a bit."

Now the chief thought. She paced to the end of the driveway, head down. On the way back, her lips formed a small smile.

"By golly, that's it," she said.

She explained to Maisie what must have happened, that the call of nature must have taken Carl from his routine so when he come back out, he forgot he hadn't filled the reservoir. The chief chattered on. She had fretted over the problem of the empty reservoir but now everything fell into place.

Maisie stood silent.

The chief returned the container of brake fluid to the shed. She asked Maisie how she was feeling. Maisie said it was hard; she had conflicting emotions. The chief told her about survivor's guilt.

"You're thinking you should've got the truck fixed yourself, you should've made sure your son got on the school bus, you should've drove him, things like that. But some things just happen."

For the first time since the deaths of her husband and son, tears formed in Maisie's eyes.

The chief asked Maisie if the boys from the lab could come by and look around, if she'd sign a release, but it was her right not to. Maisie walked to the cruiser with the chief and signed a form on a clipboard. They could come by any time. The door was never locked.

• • • •

THE THIRD THEORY OF causality, Carl's parents had touched on at the service at Moore and Sons Funeral Home and Crematory. Everyone from the lumber yard, the diner where Ma worked, and the school made an appearance. Maisie bought a dark blue dress and took most of the gray from her hair with a rinse.

Ma and Winston had stood by her in reception of the mourners in black dress and dark gray suit. Ma lived in town, at 10 Pine Street, a colonial owned by Winston, her fiancé. Ma had started wearing eyeglasses, light blue frames. Winston was six feet, big in the chest but stoop-shouldered, with thinning red hair. He wore round, gold-framed eyeglasses. They had been together for eight months and Maisie hoped it would work, this being a first marriage for both. Everyone—from the lumber yard where Carl and Winston worked, the diner where Ma worked, and the school—made an appearance.

Maisie had grown up with Ma and the occasional boyfriend, queries regarding paternity answered by "not sure" or "best not to know." Ma's own childhood had been difficult, living on squirrel meat and turnips in hard times, as she told it. She still shot squirrels out the window if they were at the bird feeder.

As for Winston, there had been gay jokes, but he was just shy with women. Ma told how he had come into the diner mid-afternoon, no customers around, Ma filling shakers and setting up tables for dinner. He had something to say, in private. He asked her out. Ma thought she'd hit the lottery: college education, salaried job, a house in town. Not a drinker.

Carl's parents had attended the service in a side clique, never coming through reception. Every so often, a glance slithered Maisie's way. Carl's uncle, from the mother's side, approached. He said, "Don't pay them no mind. They're saying you cut the brake line for the insurance money." He laughed. "They'd like to have that money themselves. Don't pay those assholes no mind."

Of course Maisie hadn't cut the brake line; the state police lab would prove that. And she had no idea that foremen at the lumber yard had term life insurance, purchased by the company. Never thought about insurance money. But the remark started Maisie's mind churning. She thought about that morning after Carl shut himself in the bathroom and saw herself walk to the kitchen utensil drawer, take out the turkey baster and easy-twist jar opener, walk to the truck with its hood up, go on tiptoe over the motor, and twist the cap off the brake fluid reservoir. She envisioned the bulb of the turkey baster collapsing under her squeeze and its tip entering the reservoir. Then the bulb expanding as her squeeze relaxed, brake fluid being sucked from the reservoir.

• • • •

MA'S DINER HAD STARTED the trouble.

The morning before the accident, Maisie had driven down to 10 Pine for a visit. She remembered finding Ma by the open dining room window cradling her single-shot Hornet, which packed a nice wallop for critters. Maisie lifted a chair from the table where Winston sat, eyes to the morning newspaper, and in silence, joined Ma at the window. Ma flicked the pupils of her eyes, pale blue like Maisie's, at the leafless maple in the backyard. Maisie spotted a gray squirrel bending the end of a branch. The squirrel leapt from the branch to Ma's bird feeder, tail streaming, and the Hornet came up.

Maisie enjoyed watching Ma in this pose of concentration, right hand around the grip of the stock, pulling the rifle into her shoulder, cheek resting against the thumb of her right hand, pushing her glasses up a fraction. Ma aimed with her right eye but kept both open. In her peripheral vision, Maisie saw the squirrel upright on its haunches, facing them, oblivious, stuffing Ma's bird feed into its cheeks. Ma let out half a breath and tightened her trigger finger until the rifle popped, a wisp of smoke at barrel's end.

From the dining room table rolled Winston's low-pitched voice.

"Did you get him, sweetie pie?"

"That varmint has stole his last grain of millet," Ma said.

Maisie stared out the window. She asked Ma what she'd be doing with the dead squirrel. Would she be eating him?

Ma gave a hoot. She'd had enough squirrel as a girl: squirrel stew, squirrel pie, squirrel fricassee.

"I'll starve before I ever eat squirrel again."

"You won't starve on my watch," said Winston, whose eyes had yet to leave the newspaper.

Ma told Maisie to bring her chair to the table. Ma stood behind Winston, hands on his shoulders. She wanted Winston to make the announcement.

A flush came to his face and tinged his ears. He smiled.

"Well," he said, "I've proposed to your ma and she's said yes."

Maisie clapped her hands and laughed. It was about time, Winston; it was about time, Ma. The two of them living in sin and all.

Ma said, "Well that's the announcement. Now I gotta get to the diner. We're shorthanded today."

"I'll come along and work a few hours," said Maisie.

Ma's face went dark. Carl didn't like that. But Maisie said she was tired of being cooped up and told what to do. She'd help at the diner until little Carl got done at school.

"Carl is sure to hear," said Ma.

At the diner, Maisie worked for tips. Men from the lumber yard came for lunch, including Tubby Smyth, another foreman. Maisie saw him at one of Ma's tables spooning apple pie à la mode. Once, she caught him looking at her and he flashed his lecherous smile.

Tubby had been a year ahead in school, same as Carl. At house parties, she abided his prurient inspections and sly comments. He wasn't the only one. A year into the marriage, Carl's demeanor changed. Maybe it was gradual; Maisie couldn't remember. It got so the slightest look or smallest comment, from Tubby or any other man, sent Carl into a smoldering fury, and when they returned home, a full rage. They stopped going to parties.

In the beginning, Carl's demeanor had been fine. He was handsome, athletic, attentive, intense. He wanted sex, but what man didn't? When they had started dating, still in high school, Ma took Maisie to the clinic for birth control pills.

After the announcement of their engagement, Maisie was at a party talking with wives and girlfriends, including Tubby's first wife. The men were in another room, and one of the wives asked when she was due.

"I'm not pregnant," said Maisie.

The wife asked why she was getting married if she didn't have to.

"Well," said Maisie, "we're in love."

The wives laughed.

Five years into the marriage, Maisie let the birth control lapse so she could have a little girl to cuddle like Ma cuddled her. The ultrasound confused her: she felt sure it showed a girl but later, Ma said no, it had always showed a boy. She heard everyone saying, "Doesn't he look like his Pa?" and "Spitting image."

• • • •

FROM THE DINER, MAISIE drove her Civic to North Road, waited, and followed the school bus to their house, a mile past what the locals called Dead Man's Curve. Coming from town, the curve was not bad, not a dead man's curve at all. Nobody had ever crashed that way. But going to town was different: downhill on a tightening curve with but a bit of gravel before hitting the trees.

Little Carl was off the bus and in his bedroom, headset on, joystick in hand. He favored *Mortal Kombat* and *Grand Theft Auto*. Nine years old. Sometimes big Carl played with him. Why didn't he do better at school if he was so clever at video games? His marks were poor through three grades and there were behavioral problems; a recent incident on the playground involved Amy Bouvoir's "pee hole." Maisie remembered it as an incident of grave concern, but Ma told her no, her remembrance was wrong; the incident did not involve touching and was not serious.

Maisie heard Carl's pickup back into the driveway. Little Carl was sitting down for dinner—pan-fried chicken with rice and peas—when big Carl came into the kitchen, green work clothes hanging from a gaunt frame, black hair askew, hazel eyes wild.

"Boy, get with your video game," he said to little Carl, who hastened to his room.

Carl grabbed Maisie by the hair and dragged her toward the bathroom. That was her remembrance, being dragged by the hair.

"Wasn't you told?" he said.

"No, Carl, don't." Maisie grabbed the door jamb but was no match for Carl's strength as she found herself forced to her knees in front of the toilet, a wide American Standard with gallons of standing water.

"Wasn't you told?" she heard again before he drove her face under water past her ears, obliterating sound and breath.

Maisie's arms flapped as Carl held her under. Her face came out of the water with Carl's upward yank.

"Showing off your cunt at the diner are you?" Still grasping her hair, Carl warned: she could be found dead from drowning in the brook out back and everyone would think it was an accident or that she had done it herself. Is that what she wanted?

• • • •

AT THE FUNERAL SERVICE, men from the lumber yard were in work clothes: dark green polished cotton, jeans and T-shirts, yellow work boots, brown work boots; some had changed to white and light blue dress shirts. Tubby wore a brown corduroy sports jacket and brown quilted tie, whose square bottom rested on his stomach.

"Those are fine caskets you got for Carl and the boy," said Tubby. He wondered about the expense.

Maisie had been looking past Tubby, hoping he would move on. She told him they weren't expensive; they were rentals.

"Rentals?"

"Sure enough," said Maisie. The end of the casket was hinged. The funeral people slid the body out and into the furnace slick as can be, and the casket was saved for the next deceased.

"Well, I'll be," said Tubby. "Ain't that something. What will you be doing with the ashes?"

"I think I'll scatter them in the brook out back."

Tubby told Maisie she shouldn't be alone. He'd come by—say, the next evening. Maisie felt a flash of faintness.

"Don't do that, Tubby."

He persisted. He'd bring a bottle. What did she like?

"Tubby, if you come near my house, I'll call the police and have you put in jail."

Tubby stepped back. As he said "Well, well" and "If that's how you feel," Maisie turned to Mrs. Mitchell, little Carl's teacher, who presented her with a large, handmade card containing sentiments from his classmates. That night, Maisie examined the card. She found Amy Bouvoir's sentiment, which read, "Good by Carl." A close inspection revealed that "by Carl" covered an erasure. Maisie was unable to make out what was erased even with her magnifying glass, but imagined the original sentiment reading, "Good riddance," or some such true feeling.

• • • •

SEVERAL WEEKS AFTER the accident, Maisie fancied herself arrested, learning that a spy drone had been overhead the day of the accident. The federal government had taken pictures of her incidentally while going after terrorists. Her lawyer argued that it was an illegal invasion of her privacy but no surprise, the government got away with it and there she was, caught red-handed with the turkey baster and easy-twist jar opener.

At the trial, a jury of six men and six women refused to convict her for big Carl. Her lawyer got her off with nullification. But what could he say about little Carl?

"Your honor. Ladies and gentlemen of the jury. Here was a boy non-redeemable, bound to grow into a monster like his pa. You know about his pa, who intimidated everyone and beat his wife. Let me tell you about this boy." He enumerated the behavioral problems, the violent video games, the talking back, the "pee-hole" incident.

The jury didn't buy it and Maisie was sent to the women's prison at Goffstown. There, she met Pamela Smart, who commiserated with her. Pamela had been convicted many years earlier for masterminding the murder of her husband.

She said, "It's so unfair. Even if I did it, they didn't prove it. Look at the transcript. They didn't prove it."

Then Maisie remembered that Pamela Smart had been transferred to a prison in New York years ago and was no longer at Goffstown. Maisie looked about her. She wasn't at Goffstown; she was standing in her kitchen. She felt her arms. She felt her legs. She deduced that the drone, the trial, prison—all of it—had not happened.

It was early evening. Maisie drove down to see Ma. Winston turned off the television news and joined them at the dining room table.

Maisie told Ma about her recollection of being arrested for tampering with the truck. She told Ma about the trial and the women's prison at Goffstown. She told Ma about her conversation with Pamela Smart.

"Oh goodness," Ma said. Her eyes watered. She moved her chair next to Maisie's, put her arm around her daughter's shoulders, pulled her close.

Winston sat open-mouthed.

Ma said, "Sometimes Maisie gets these awful dreams."

"They're not dreams," said Maisie. "They're remembrances."

"Remembrances," said Ma. "But they never happened."

"Sometimes they did."

Ma kissed Maisie on the forehead and got up to close the dining room window. Maisie's gaze followed Ma. The window had a screen and outside, Maisie saw neither maple tree nor bird feeder.

"Ma," said Maisie, "the morning I come over and worked in the diner, was you shooting a squirrel out the window?"

Both Winston's and Ma's faces went from concern to bursts of laughter.

Winston said, "I've heard tales of that squirrel gun."

Ma said, "Honey, I got rid of that Hornet years ago. Why, the police would be at the door if I was shooting a gun in town."

"Well then," said Maisie. "That morning, did you and Winston announce your engagement?"

"Why we did, sure enough. And you made a joke about living in sin."

"Sure enough," said Maisie.

• • • •

MAISIE DROVE BACK UP North Road, sat at the kitchen table, turned the matter over in her mind. She could imagine killing big Carl, could imagine that being real. Not little Carl, though. That was impossible. Wasn't it? Here was the problem: she didn't miss him; she was relieved he was gone; she was relieved she didn't have to deal with him anymore, would not have to deal with him as a teenager, would not have to deal with him grown up.

Maisie opened the utensil drawer. She would examine the physical evidence. She would know one way or the other.

She located the easy-twist jar opener and examined it under bright light with her magnifying glass. No signs of oil or brake fluid. No grime. She smelled it. Nothing. Of course, she would have washed it afterward, although that wasn't in her remembrance.

Next Maisie searched for the turkey baster. She dumped the utility drawer onto the kitchen table. She searched the other kitchen drawers. She searched the trash. She went outside and searched the shed. Nowhere to be found. Did she dispose of it? No remembrance.

As Maisie pondered, a text message from the police chief appeared on her phone. Could she drop by the station in the morning?

• • • •

IN THE MORNING, MAISIE thought of fleeing. Get her hands on the insurance money and flee, out west, or to the Caribbean Islands. She drank coffee, spread jam on toast. The getaway thoughts passed. At nine, she drove down to the town offices.

The police station had its own one-story brick building with a small public area inside the front door. The dispatcher buzzed her through a second door and led her down a hall to the chief's office. The chief waved Maisie to a chair on the other side of her cluttered desk. Paperwork, a coffee cup, newspapers, folders, more paperwork, a laptop, the chief's hat, and in a clear plastic bag, Maisie's turkey baster.

The chief pushed papers toward Maisie, then caught the fix of her eyes.

"You knew we took that, didn't you?"

Maisie shook her head.

"We left a form. On the kitchen table."

Maisie hadn't read it. The chief apologized. She explained. Two boys from State had inspected her property, with the chief in attendance. She assured Maisie that the inspection was above board and neat. They left a form saying what they had done and what they had taken for lab work.

Maisie was still staring at the plastic bag. The chief said, look, she'd tell Maisie the story in a minute. She chuckled; it was a good story. But first, she needed Maisie's signature for the returned evidence and pushed across a pen. Maisie signed and dated the bottom of three forms, put down the pen, and looked across to the chief's eyes.

The chief pointed to the turkey baster. She shook her head and launched into a tale, how the boys at State watched too many reruns of *Law & Order* and *CSI: Crime Scene Investigation*, how they decided to investigate the accident as a possible homicide, how the prime suspect, as always, was the spouse. Next, they tried to figure out how the spouse did it. The chief accompanied the story with eye rolls, shoulder shrugs, arm waves, and bursts of laughter.

The boys were snooping around Maisie's kitchen, opening drawers. One of them saw the turkey baster.

"So this state police detective says, he actually says, 'That's how she done it! She sucked the fluid out with the turkey baster.'"

The chief fell back in her chair laughing. She told Maisie the boys insisted on taking the turkey baster, dropped it into an evidence bag for examination at the lab. Said it was almost impossible to have washed it clean. There would be some residue of brake fluid. All they needed was a speck.

The chief looked at Maisie's face.

"I'm sorry. I guess you don't find this funny. It's just those boys at State, when brains were handed out.... Well, I shouldn't be talking out of school."

The chief stood. Maisie stood. They shook hands. The chief handed Maisie the turkey baster.

"I guess they didn't find no residue," said Maisie.

The chief laughed and pulled tissues from the desk clutter. She wiped tears from her eyes. She blew her nose.

"I guess they didn't."

The Pugilist

As the rear door clicked behind him, Carlos shook off an assault of cold night air. Early fall in New England: pleasant days but chilly nights. His wife sat in front of him on the edge of the cement stoop, feet planted on the second step, a green cardigan draped over her shoulders. Linda from the townhouse to the left sat next to his wife wrapped in a dark blue blanket she'd carted over. Linda Snoop sat on a stoop minding her neighbor's poop. Along came—. Carlos blanked on his wife's name, hated when that happened, feared uttering the wrong name, an old girlfriend or a current fantasy. Ana, that's it. Along came Ana who plopped down beside her. Hmm, but didn't scare her away.

Beyond the two women lay a non-bucolic panorama. Short patches of lawn, a line of cars parked head in, and across the parking lot two dumpsters, brown and green. Past the parking lot, hardwood trees and scrub pine, silhouettes in the current darkness, strewn with paper cups and plastic wrappers in daylight. Above the trees, a scattering of stars, those with enough radiance to break through the haze of the overhead street lamps.

Carlos shook off a second stab from the night air. "What are you doing?" he said.

Without turning, Linda from next door said, "Shh."

Ana leaned back with upturned face and whispered, "Listening to the fight."

Now that Carlos knew, he realized he'd been hearing an altercation since he stepped out, its venue two units to the right. The combatants were Gabe, a big guy older than Carlos, and his wife Joyce, younger than Carlos, raven hair, a hot number. Wife and husband exchanged insults with fervor, soprano versus bass, but Carlos couldn't discern the words that Ana and Linda leaned forward to pluck. Non-vocal sounds entered the fray—breaking dishes.

"Should we call the cops?"

"Shh," said Linda.

Ana again leaned back with upturned face. "Don't be an ass. It's just getting good."

Another shiver. Carlos reversed direction, opened the back door, and stepped into his kitchen of red linoleum, silver appliances, and a breakfast counter that jutted toward him from the opposite wall. Three stools ran the length of the counter, and one anchored the short side. Carlos leaned against the short-side stool with his left hand and adjusted his ears to the interior of the house: all quiet. He considered checking on the kids, but … best leave well enough alone. He'd tucked them in with the Berenstain Bears—Carlos eyeballed the digital clock on the counter—a while ago. He'd waited, checked, waited, and checked again before igniting a stogie of sinsemilla cannabis and taking two deep hits, his goal a mild buzz, not a blitz. So much for good intentions.

Twisting and placing the small of his back against the counter, left hand still on the end stool, Carlos hoped his mother wouldn't call. The kitchen lay in twilight, its lights off, the only illumination drifting in from a lamp on the living room end table and a 60-watt bulb in the overhead hallway fixture. He hated when his mother called and he was high. She'd say, Carlos, is everything okay? You don't seem yourself. Is everything alright with you and Ana? Carlos, talk to me. Are you there?

What was happening outside? Must be cold—Linda Snoop-de-doop had a blanket wrapped around her. Oh, right, Gabe, and his hot wife, Joyce, going at it again. What if it really got out of hand? What if he started whacking her? That angered Carlos, Gabe beating on Joyce, and Carlos imagined himself intervening. As Ana and Linda screamed and dialed nine-one-one, Carlos strode across the intervening backyard, mounted Gabe and Joyce's rear stoop, and pushed their door open without knocking. Joyce cowered in the far corner of the kitchen; Gabe turned to confront Carlos. Gabe had him on height and muscle, but Carlos didn't care, raised his fists and danced in front of his heavyweight opponent. Gabe advanced, left fist up and right cocked. Carlos jabbed with his left, catching the cocky giant under the eye, feeling the blow to his elbow, knowing if the punch hurt him, he'd done damage to his opponent. Gabe backed off a step with a stunned gaze, then bared his teeth and stepped forward only to meet another jab, this one to the nose. Fury engulfed Gabe's face as he set himself for a charge. Carlos faded sideways then stepped forward and buried his right fist in Gabe's midriff. Oomph, said Gabe as his knees buckled, but the murder in his eyes told Carlos the fight was far from finished.

Carlos danced backward on his toes, scissoring his legs, fists up. He lunged forward, still scissoring his legs, and jammed his right knee on the breakfast counter end stool. Dropping his boxer's stance, Carlos bent from the waist and grabbed the top of the stool with both hands. For a second, the high seat, tilted on two legs, held, but as center of gravity shifted, it fell sideways, depositing Carlos butt down on the red linoleum.

The kitchen door flew open. Carlos, on the floor with splayed legs and a tumbled stool, observed the advancing knees of Ana's khaki culottes. He raised his eyes to her face.

"Carlos, what the fuck are you doing?"

While Carlos pushed on the floor with his right hand in a futile effort to rise, Ana bent over, grabbed the stool, and set it back on its legs.

"Have you been smoking?"

As prelude to a second attempt to rise, Carlos rolled sideways to his hands and knees.

"Jesus," said Ana, "we don't have to listen to Joyce and numb nuts. We've got it right here."

Using the stool for leverage, almost upsetting it again, Carlos dragged himself to his feet.

"It's a little embarrassing, you know," said Ana. "Linda's out there laughing her ass off." Ana walked past Carlos into the hall, turned, and returned. "It's a wonder you didn't wake them up."

Carlos wanted to provide an explanation but couldn't gather his thoughts much less piece them into coherent discourse. As he struggled for remnants of an excuse, he noticed Ana had disappeared, that the outside door had closed and clicked. Carlos turned, banged again against the end stool, and grabbed the counter for support. He had to evacuate this dangerous place, this minefield. With deliberate steps, stopping only to snag a 4-ounce bag of Fritos Original, Carlos changed his environs from kitchen to living room. There he slumped onto the end of the sofa away from the lamp. On the positive side, the kids were still asleep, and his mother hadn't called. And Ana would get over it. Carlos pulled open the mustard and red bag in his hands, placed a chip on his tongue, savoring salt and corn, and drew it between his teeth. Crunch. Mmm.

His imagined bout with Gabe, Carlos now realized: how phony; how unrealistic. He would never beat that giant in a fight. He might prance around him and get in a jab, but one blow from Gabe would crush him. Carlos saw himself on their kitchen floor, blood dribbling from his lower lip, Gabe above him with balled fists. And Joyce ... and Joyce dropping to her knees, her right arm over his prone body, her left hand held in the air against Gabe. Get out, she yelled. Look what you've done, get out. And Gabe ... and Gabe yelling back, all right, bitch, I'm out of here. The kitchen door opened and closed. Carlos heard a motor, the clashing of gears, the squealing of tires. Oh my God, said Joyce, holding Carlos with both arms, let me kiss that blood away. As their lips met, Carlos slipped a tentative right hand under the back of her blouse and touched the clips of her bra strap. It's okay, she said with a slight separation of their lips, I want it as much as you.

"Carlos." A loud whisper from between kitchen and living room, Ana, outlined by the overhead light from the hallway. "What's the deal? You coming to bed tonight?"

• • • •

CARLOS WASN'T SURE which hurt more, the high pitch of his three-year-old daughter's voice or its excessive volume. "Mine!" she screeched.

His son, two years older, retorted an octave lower but with equal volume. "It is not yours. It is a family bowl."

"The pink bowl," Carlos began to say, but a remonstration from the bathroom cut him off.

"Carlos, can't you deal with them for ten minutes?"

"Mine!"

A quarter of an hour later, Carlos walked out the back door, hastened down the walkway, and moved the car seat and booster seat from his ten-year-old Hyundai to Ana's SUV. Her day for transport. Carlos settled behind the wheel of the Hyundai with a straight-on view of his rear stoop, and, as he turned the ignition key, saw Gabe stepping out onto his stoop. The motor started with an elongated chirping noise. Gotta have that looked at.

What's this? Gabe, instead of heading straight to his own car, was walking diagonally across the narrow patches of rear lawn toward Carlos. For seconds, Carlos denied the reality of the behemoth's advance. What could he want? Last night Carlos imagined fisticuffs with Gabe, but they didn't occur in real life. Last night, Carlos imagined fucking Gabe's wife, but—. He must have seen Ana and Linda sitting on the stoop snooping, that's it. Maybe he even saw Carlos.

It struck Carlos that not only was Gabe older but of a different generation. Ten or fifteen additional years with deep creases to his face, horizontal on the forehead, vertical about the cheeks, and more bounce to his midriff. And of a different class, a street-wise blue-collar grunt, jeans and yellow work boots.

At the driver's side of the Hyundai, Gabe twirled his finger like an old-time window crank. To himself, Carlos said, fuck me, then lowered the glass that separated him from Gabe. Gabe pointed a thick, hairy finger toward the front of the car and said, "Pop the hood."

"What's that?" said Carlos looking up.

"Pop the hood, buddy, and kill the motor."

Carlos obeyed, pulling the hood release and turning the ignition key counterclockwise. Gabe looked around from the raised hood and beckoned. Again Carlos obeyed, opening the driver's door, stepping out, stepping forward, and facing his neighbor over the exposed motor of the car.

Gabe flicked Carlos on the chest with the fingers of his right hand. "What the hell?" he said.

Carlos wet his lips.

Gabe pointed into the motor compartment. "Jesus Christ, buddy, look at that fan belt."

Carlos stared into the cavern formed by the raised hood. Gabe was pointing at a black, serpentine cincture to the front of the motor. "Not gonna last another hundred."

Carlos lifted his eyes from the mystery compartment. "Yeah, I've been meaning to—."

"Look," said Gabe, "grab one today. We'll throw it in tonight."

Carlos said, "I couldn't—"

"Won't take twenty minutes. Target down the street."

"What's that?"

"Target. Go to the auto department." The cavern disappeared as Gabe slammed the hood shut. "You're Carlos, right? What's that, Rican?"

Carlos nodded.

Gabe pushed his finger into his own chest. "Fucking Greek." He lifted his chin toward the back door to Carlos's house. "Old lady and kids, eh?"

"Yeah, two."

Gabe lifted his chin toward the back door of his house. "None this time around. Just the old lady." Gabe laughed. "That's enough. What's her name again, your old lady?"

"Ana."

"Nice looking. You ever wanna swap some night, let me know."

What the holy fuck?

Gabe balled his right hand into a fist and punched Carlos on the left shoulder. "Just joking, buddy." He laughed. "Should see your face. Tell me, you ever get into it with her?"

"We're okay. Yeah, I mean, sometimes there's an argument."

"Mine, Joyce, she can really push your buttons. Last night ... surprised the cops weren't over. Or that nosy broad the other side of youse, what's her name?"

"Linda."

"Yeah, what a piece of work."

Carlos pointed through his windshield. "Look, I have to—"

"Yeah, me too."

Carlos stepped toward the door of his car but found his chest blocked by Gabe's right hand. Gabe released the hand but raised its forefinger.

"Don't forget the belt."

Sunrise Cliff

Erin and Ernie had been lovers for seven years. To rekindle their romance, the couple undertook a predawn pilgrimage to Sunrise Cliff, renowned for its autumnal beauty. The promontory, facing east over a sheer drop of 800 feet, opened to a panorama of multi-colored wilderness below and hills beyond. Viewed best at dawn. Ernie led the way, negotiating the uphill track on the cliff's wooded western slope with his customary assertiveness, his boots finding the firmest hold at every step in the cone of light from his headlamp. Erin followed with less enthusiasm, this climb a microcosm of their life, seven years of headlong rush that never slowed to enjoy the moment.

Erin's boot slipped sideways on a slanted root, and she fell to one knee. With more annoyance than concern, Ernie called back, "You alright?"

"Yes. Keep going. Don't want to get off our precious schedule."

"No need for sarcasm."

Up the path floated added commentary from Erin. "You know, we're supposed to be rekindling."

"Right," came the downhill rejoinder, "but how does that happen if we don't get there on time? We have—" Ernie looked at the fluorescent hands of his watch. "—eighteen minutes."

The couple surged upward and, with four minutes to spare, broke from the woods, their headlamps probing the jagged eastern drop-off. Beyond the void, the onset of dawn back-lit distant hilltops.

"Shall we?" said Ernie. He switched off his lamp and approached the edge of the cliff, stopping a foot from its vertical eighth-of-a-mile plunge. He edged his boots forward another few inches, as far as his puckering posterior allowed.

Erin wet her lips and followed, halting at Ernie's right. Her left hand found the small of his back as Ernie settled his right palm on her right shoulder blade. The sky shifted from midnight blue to morning azure. A moment later, the sun peered over the distant hills, setting the lowlands aglow in yellows and reds, and splashing splendor on the barren face of Sunrise Cliff.

Ole Ned

The release chopper hovered over abandoned land, near former Philadelphia. Lucius listened to the count of the crew chief, "three," "two," "godspeed," and slid out the rear hatch with a bearing of one-eighty. Twenty-two hundred hours, no moon.

He flew a Powered Stealth Glider, preferred for deploying an Immigration Deterrent Agent (IDA) in the 2080s. Little more than Syrotex super cloth, composite struts, and a small rear motor, meant for three hours of flight then disposed of. Lucius coasted a hundred meters above the swampland at a hundred twenty kilometers per hour. A LectroMap controlled navigation, signals turned off to avoid detection, maps having been updated that afternoon. He hung below the glider head forward like a bat, silent, the small hum from the motor drowned by the squawks and burps of the fetidness beneath.

Lucius was a veteran, his sixth mission, missions lasting four to six weeks—Border Security gave the agents wide latitude. How many more? He didn't know, could opt out any time, no questions, no recriminations, take a cozy outpost out west, Idaho, Montana, or a staff slot in Toronto. Most agents got out after four because of the casualty rate, twenty-one percent per mission, calculating four times twenty-one made eighty-four and the next mission put you over. Superstition. The rules of probability reset the clock each mission, always twenty-one.

Lucius wore the latest survival suit, a double layer of Syrotex with sandwiched electronics for cooling and varmint repulsion. The electronics recharged through heat and motion. Syrotex was ultra-light, waterproof, breathable, self-cleaning, and almost indestructible. From the neck down, the camouflaged outfit rode close to the body protecting every millimeter, but for the latest suits, the Model G's, the masterstroke was the automated waste elimination system with integrated bidet. Lucius still found it incredible he could crap his pants and moments later be clean and tidy. Hats off to the engineering wonks of Border Security.

An oval Plastex helmet fastened at the neck. It appeared camouflage from the outside but from the inside gave all-around visibility with UV protection, adaptive tinting, night vision, and magnification to 40x. The helmet contained read-outs for maps and materials, including leisure—Border Security let the agents take whatever they wanted. All controlled by pupil movement and blinks.

The motor stopped. Nylon cord unfurled and Lucius rappelled into green-black water to his chest, buoyancy tubes arresting his sinking. He hand-paddled until under canopy with feet touching. Soon he was slogging on a knee-deep path, felt like an old macadam road.

Lucius was in top physical condition, training administered by automated stress and aerobic machines. An IDA not up to snuff at mission time was scrubbed.

Lucius was smart. He held bachelor and graduate degrees. Border Security didn't want gorillas, wanted agents to think, do no more popping than necessary.

Lucius approached his objective, a narrow north-south oasis, a strip of high ground with a spring-fed brook, a favorite squatting spot for illegals. It was evening. Lucius found a cozy spot in the crook of a cypress, inflated his integrated mattress, turned in for the night, woke with the sun at his back. He watched the oasis for a while, zoomed, scanned, checked his sensors. Around four hundred illegals, meaning four or five armed smugglers guiding them.

Lucius waded into chest-deep water, reduced buoyancy, and squatted to neck level, could go under if need be. He advanced toward the near shoreline of the oasis taking an hour to cover a hundred meters. He zoomed and found a smuggler on sentry duty at the south end of the land mass and another further north. They wore obsolete Model B suits without gloves or helmets.

With a blink and pupil shift, Lucius activated the Glytox Automatic Acquisition Ground Weapon System, the latest in individual armament. Its magazine curved down the back of Lucius's helmet while the chamber and barrel poked out the top. Lucius acquired the sentry on the kill screen, put a laser dot on his forehead, and gave the blink. The Glytox made no noise, not even a swoosh. The sentry dropped.

Lucius turned his head to the right, acquired the second smuggler, and fired. The smuggler fell sideways but this time a cry went up. Lucius sank to eye level and moved north.

Bullets splatted the swamp water where Lucius had been. Old-style automatic rifles—lots of noise, no acquisition systems.

Lucius completed a flanking maneuver coming ashore north of the illegals. He discerned fire from three rifles, moved south, located one smuggler then beyond a second. They were looking east into the swamp, into the sun, firing bursts. Lucius dropped them with pops to the sides of their heads.

He moved toward the downed men. Illegals appeared to his right, a mixed crowd, half women, many kids, all ages. The third rifleman exited the vegetation and threw down his weapon. Lucius popped him in the forehead.

The illegals screamed and ran. They ran south, mothers holding children, couples holding hands. Lucius scanned for weapons. He let stragglers take their time, let them gather belongings, fill water bottles. He checked to the north, checked along the brook, trailed the crowd as they floundered south, checked their flanks for strays, did not have to pop anyone else.

Lucius rolled the smuggler remains into the swamp along with the antiquated weapons. He scanned the oasis, first along the brook, then the west side of the brook, then back to the larger eastern piece. He searched up an old road dotted with pieces of tar. An alert from the sensors. Lucius moved to the corner of a cellar hole and looked down on a human, prone, stomach down. Bollocks, he thought, just what I don't need, an up-close stay-behind. Lucius activated the Glytox and set a dot on short, black hair just above the human's nape.

Lucius thought back three weeks to a farewell party for an IDA who had tossed it in, announced his last mission. Fellow agents gathered at his apartment, whiskey and beer flowing, taboo topics drifting into the conversation. The outgoing IDA, his voice up, opined that balking at a close-in popping constituted not so much a breach of operating procedures—whiskey slopping over and dribbling on his fingers—but the hanging onto of a shred of humanity. There followed a few small laughs.

On the fringe of the conversation drifted Jane, Lucius's supervisor, blond with streaks of gray, two missions before going administrative, so not without standing among the IDAs. Lucius had taken a seat on the retiring agent's divan and Jane joined him, hip to hip, knee to knee.

"Jane, you're a terrible flirt."

"Lou," said Jane, "I do hope you're not going soft on us."

Lucius extended an arm toward the remnants of the conversation. "Just boy chatter."

"You must keep to your training. The ten-one rule."

"Jane, can't you see we're in the midst of a party?"

"Right, but I do hope you won't forget your ten-one."

The wonks had determined that outside ten meters IDAs could be trained to treat humans as action figures, as in a simulator. That was the first part of ten-one—never get within ten meters. The second part was to not procrastinate, to place the dot and give the blink within one second of ascertaining target.

Lucius jumped into the cellar and nudged the human's calf with his boot. A woman rolled on her back, his age, white swamp sneakers, light blue Plynthetic pants, white top of the same material, breasts rising and falling. She had wide nostrils and brown eyes set apart, more resigned than scared. Lucius thought, well, if I've gone this far, might as well be hospitable, and formed a smile until he remembered, of course, she couldn't see through the camouflaged helmet.

"Say, love," he said, "why don't we head across to the brook. Nicer there."

Her breasts still heaved. "Then what?"

"Then we'll have a chat. C'mon, now. You can't stay here. And can't be going into the swamp on your own. Right then?"

At the brook, the woman slipped into a pool formed by a small waterfall, held her head under, emerged. Lucius sat on the brook's edge. "Here's the thing," he said. "I don't mind you hanging about if you're not a nuisance. We can set you up with a little hut or whatnot. But I need some assurances."

Lucius brought both hands to his neckline, pulled the quick-release, and lifted his helmet away. He felt the rush of heat and humidity, breathed in a wisp of cool from the brook.

"Can I have some assurances then?"

"Why you're Black like me."

Lucius relaxed his shoulders. He formed a small smile. "Nobody up north takes notice of race."

"Course they do. Everybody does."

"No, they really don't," said Lucius. "No more than hair color."

"Go on. Nobody stands out?"

"Well," said Lucius, "Newfies maybe."

The girl narrowed her eyes.

"It's a joke," said Lucius. "What's your name?"

Lucius had a mahogany face and skull, round, and—at this stage of the mission—bare, it being the practice for agents to shave hair and beard before going out. The inside of his lips glimmered red when he smiled. The woman was a darker brown.

"Clara," she said.

"Lovely name. Call me Lou."

"Um, Lou. What do you get out of this arrangement?"

"Sex is not an issue if that's your meaning."

"Not an issue?"

"Right. Regulations prohibit sex on missions. It's a bore, I know, but management is quite adamant. There's been meetings and such."

Clara's head tilted back in the water and her eyes roamed the sky. "You're watched every minute then."

"There's no minders," said Lucius. "No signals in or out until mission's end. But that actually reinforces the need for proper behavior. Don't you see?"

"Lou, I've never known a man with proper behavior. But maybe that's why you northern folk got the upper hand."

"Not at all, it's geography, Clara, geography that did you. Where are you from then?"

"Atlanta. Or where Atlanta used to be."

"Relations?"

"Not anymore. So I just hang out here while you do your thing? Stay out of trouble?"

Lucius gave her the nod.

"What happens at the end? When you're done here?"

"Ah, a thorny issue."

"Is it true they'll execute me if I go on up there and I'm found out."

"You wouldn't go up there. You wouldn't make it. But, yes, the immigration policy is quite cut-and-dried."

"I don't understand that. Aren't y'all supposed to be this bastion of civility? Where everyone's taken care of?"

"Quite so. For citizens."

Clara's eyes had teared. She oscillated her arms to maintain balance in the brook.

"It's a matter of dire necessity," said Lucius. "Even up north we're losing habitable land at an alarming rate. All we can do to take care of ourselves, don't you see?"

• • • •

LUCIUS HAD NOT PROVIDED Clara complete intelligence. Proper behavior had not overridden sexual desire. What happened was early on Border Security tagged as high severity what they called (with bureaucratic indelicacy) the "masturbatory issue" or, when illegals became involved, the "fornicatory issue." Brainstorming ensued. The wonks suggested a chemical solution, implanting in outgoing agents a slow-release Exosterone tablet, just enough to impede libido. Senior male staff objected, countering that operational efficacy would plummet, favoring an in-suit stimulation solution along the lines of waste removal. There were angry rants—"cutting their balls off" and such.

Lucius recalled a lunch date with Jane, just the two of them, a decent place, bottle of white half gone. She was reconstructing a meeting of the division bigwigs over Exosterone, mimicking Archie, their division chief, swinging a spoon to her front, pouting her lips, pushing her teeth out: "How can they be popping illegals if we're taking their testes?" On a refrain of "taking their testes," Jane tumbled her wine glass, then lost balance and slid from her chair to a sitting position on the floor still swinging the spoon. A fine lunch, thought Lucius, then pondered lady agents, could do with more ladies in the field, but they just didn't have the same predilection for popping as the boys.

The chemical solution, easy to implement and cheap, went to testing. To the chagrin of senior male staff, Exosterone appeared to enhance agent performance, in addition to achieving the desired libido effect. Like most agents, Lucius didn't mind Exosterone, in fact, found life in the field more agreeable without a nagging sexual appetite, knowing it would return within a few weeks of mission's end. The agents adapted. Traditions and jokes evolved, raising the flag at mission's end and so forth.

As for his off-hand, illiberal remark regarding Newfies, well, it held more than a grain of truth. The Newfoundlanders in Border Security stood out. Lucius wasn't sure why, whether it was the slant of their teeth, the slant of their heads, the slant of their words, the way their eyes wandered. Perhaps because the encroaching seas had all but obliterated their homeland. An odd lot.

Ole Ned came off as the oddest. Nickname of course, real name Edwin or Edgar Something.

He'd entered the service before Lucius's time, enlisting from Grand Falls-Windsor (in the middle of the island, high, secure yet), went out with the initial wave of agents, completed ten missions, a record, and vanished on the eleventh.

Lucius had seen Ole Ned in the flesh his fourth week of basic IDA training. It was between missions ten and eleven for Ned. The training staff had brought him in as a specimen of experience, to tell the recruits what it was like in the wild. The recruits asked how do you stand it for weeks at a time, the heat, the water, the critters, the insects?

"It's not so bad," said Ned. "It grows on you."

The recruits laughed.

A year after he failed to rendezvous, rumors floated that Ned was alive, couldn't kill a Newfie, had gone native. It became a running joke. When an IDA came in from the field, other agents asked not how did it go but, "Did you see Ole Ned? How's he doing?" The returning IDA would reply, "Why Ned he's looking fine. Hale as can be."

Two agents (that Lucius knew of) had gone over the edge, insisted it wasn't a joke, that Ole Ned was out there, they had seen him up close, spoken with him. They were given medical discharges under section 64.

• • • •

STORMS ROILED FOR FIVE days. At dawn of day six, Lucius left the encampment and waded west to the southern tip of a smaller oasis, little more than roots and vegetation resting on swamp water. An alligator swam his way, felt the anti-varmint vibrations, turned back. The smaller oasis interdicted a known immigration trail. Late morning the sensors picked up movement to the south, a swarm of human bodies. Mid-afternoon the illegals came into view hip and waist deep in the green murk.

Lucius counted two smugglers and eight illegals abreast before him, many more behind, over a hundred. At two hundred meters, Lucius popped the smuggler on the left. As he sank away, the smuggler on the right hid behind an illegal, yelled for them to keep advancing. Tentative steps lurched the mass closer. Lucius popped the closest two. He then popped the illegal being used as a shield and took out the smuggler. Another smuggler was making his way forward in the mass. Lucius picked him off.

The illegals backed away, turned around. Lucius tracked their retreat for another hour before returning to the home oasis.

"You look awful," said Clara.

Lucius had submerged his body in the brook and pulled off his helmet.

"Do you want some tea? Natural ingredients."

"I could do with a spot."

"You've got a stressful job, Lou, shooting folk. How'd you get into it?"

"We call it popping. You know how it goes. I was young. It seemed like an adventure. Once I was in, well, peer pressure and all that. My, that's a fine cup of tea, Clara."

"Boys like popping, don't they, Lou?"

"They do, Clara. In the beginning." Lucius put his lips to the cup and drew away some tea. "But it's important to keep in mind the dire necessity. There's no other way."

"When you get done here, what happens?"

"Oh, I'm choppered out along with my backup." Clara squinted. "We're tiered. My backup is Al, nice chap, second mission." Lucius jutted his chin. "About twenty clicks north of here."

"Will you be shooting me before you leave?"

"It's popping, Clara, and I really don't think I could do that. Even if it were in your best interest."

• • • •

TWO NIGHTS LATER LUCIUS came awake to the vibration of the sensors. Something big slithering his way. Lucius applied night vision, zoomed, could not get a visual. The sensors indicated less than ten meters.

A whisper undulated across the low-lying night air. "Don't be doing anything rash, lad."

Lucius recognized the voice. Feck me arse, he thought, is it a section 64 then? "Ned?"

In response, a chuckle.

At dawn, Lucius zoomed and scanned.

"Easy as she goes, lad." And the apparition rose from ferns and moss.

From basic training, Lucius remembered an imposing mortal a hand under two meters with thick red hair, trimmed beard and mustaches, and pale blue eyes below bushy brows. There was no doubt from its stature and crooked face that here stood the same life form, but head and facial hair had gone gray, still thick, untrimmed, flowing past shoulders, beard past the navel, mustaches obscuring the mouth.

He wore thin shorts and a sleeveless pull-over. On his back rested a small rucksack and hanging from that an old AK-2047-W assault rifle. They were rugged weapons. They could be held underwater (hence the W), banged against rocks, would still fire. They had 128-round magazines, but were noisy, inaccurate, no acquisition system.

Ned looked around.

"Got a playmate, I see."

He dropped the rucksack and rifle, sat down, and pulled out ready meals. Lucius removed his helmet.

Ned asked how the hunting was going. Lucius told him about the group he'd chased off the oasis at the beginning of the mission, the group he'd turned back the day previous.

Ned said, "I'll show you another route they're using. Not on your maps yet."

They munched their meals. Lucius asked, wasn't it hot out there without a survival suit? Wasn't the air turgid? Wasn't it lonely?

An hour later, Ned led the way off the home oasis, southwest, then west, swamp and cypress, waist and chest deep. Lucius couldn't imagine being without a suit. Ned in shorts and sandals. Alligators approached him, turned away. They went through a thicket of black wasps. The insects split like the Red Sea before Moses.

About noon Ned stopped. Lucius said the new route didn't look like much. Ned said they were getting desperate. There was a group coming up, would be here soon. Lucius checked his sensors, zoomed to the south, found nothing.

Mid-afternoon the sensors came alive. Ned said he would go southwest a few hundred meters taking their left flank. Wait for his move, he said, and disappeared into the swamp water. Lucius saw him come up for a gulp of air eighty meters out. Then he went under again.

The illegals came into view at four hundred meters. Lucius sank in the swamp to eye level, his camouflage helmet merging with the slime.

Three hundred meters. A smuggler to the front, a smuggler on the western flank. A large group, eight to the rank. Lucius couldn't tell how deep.

Two hundred meters.

The group had waded forward another fifty meters when Ned rose to his waist on their flank with screams and gunfire, slime pasting his gray hair and beard to face and body. Under his mustaches an abyss expiated the pierce of a swamp raven. The AK-2047-W chattered to the sky with flame and smoke.

The illegals turned and ran as best they could in murk to their waists and chests. Some dove and swam. They dropped packs. The smugglers ran too, in fact, led the retreat. Lucius didn't blame them. He would have run himself.

Ned was rummaging through dropped packs that had yet to sink when Lucius waded up to him. Ready meals, knives, bullets, electronics, narcotics, distilled spirits. Ned hummed as he selected and discarded.

"You see," he said, "no need to be popping anyone. Just give 'em the wee scare."

Ned continued to hum, select, discard. Then tossing his head toward the home oasis. "What's to become of your sweetheart?"

Lucius disclosed a vague plan. Inserting Clara into a group of illegals being turned back.

"Lovely," said Ned.

Ned evaporated on the way back to the home oasis.

Next morning Lucius lowered himself in the brook and removed his helmet. He pulled off his gloves and beckoned to Clara. They squatted a meter apart in the water butterflying their arms.

Lucius said, "Your chances of making it north and surviving are twenty percent. Do you want to give it a go?"

"How do you get twenty percent?"

"Ah," said Lucius, "our guest of yesterday, the gentleman with the white beard, he'll clear some hurdles. Otherwise your chances would be zero."

Ned would drop in on Al, the backup IDA, Lucius explained, have a word. That would get Clara out of the border lands into the abandoned lands. The abandoned lands were dotted with abolitionist outposts. Clara knew of the abolitionists? So-called because they advocated an end to the zero-immigration policy and the popping of illegals. They were known to pick up strays who made it past the agents, provide forged identities and transport north. Ned would drop in, have them keep a lookout.

"Then shouldn't my odds be better?"

"Many obstacles," said Lucius. "Twenty kilometers to navigate on your own. And we don't know about Al, whether he'll really let you through. Whether you'll find the abolitionist outpost. Whether they can set you up. Not be under government surveillance."

"Many obstacles," said Clara.

"And if you make it through, the rest of your life is on guard. The slightest mistake and you're all done. Suppose you made it through and one day saw me. What would you do?"

Clara shook her head.

"Not a thing," said Lucius. "Too dangerous to even give a glance. And you've got to lose that accent."

Clara smiled. "You mean, roight then, mate, instead of y'all, mate?"

Lucius wasn't smiling. "Don't you see this is a matter of life or death?"

Lucius handed Clara a LectroMap lifted from an illegal's pack. He demonstrated its use, how to find her way on the ground without sending out signals. He had her memorize the location of an abolitionist outpost.

"What happens if they catch me? Will there be—an interrogation?"

Lucius took her hands. They had the feel of electricity at low voltage.

"Actually, it's quite civilized. You'll never know what happened."

• • • •

CLARA LEFT THE FOLLOWING morning. A month later the mission was up. Lucius tramped north and put out a signal. Al responded and they linked up at the extraction point, pulled off helmets, Lucius with fifteen millimeters of black hair and beard, Al coated in reddish brown. They lounged, waiting for the chopper. Protocol was to not compare notes, to be debriefed separately.

But a bit of banter was permissible.

"Did you get a glimpse of Ole Ned then?" said Lucius.

"Sure enough," said Al, "and he's looking grand."

• • • •

LUCIUS WENT OUT TWICE more. He took great care with the ten-one rule and never dealt again with a close-up situation. He relocated often avoiding another night encounter with Ole Ned, or maybe Ole Ned didn't fancy a second visit.

On the last mission, on the last group, they kept coming. He popped two smugglers at two hundred meters. He popped two illegals. They didn't stop. They were eight and ten abreast. Lucius popped everyone in the first rank. As they sank, the second rank walked over them. Lucius popped everyone in the second rank.

At eighty meters they stopped, the rear ranks banging into the front, milling about, looking in his direction, looking back.

When Lucius put in his release-from-active request, Jane had him up for the mandatory chat. She sat behind her faux maple desk with brushed stainless legs. Lucius took a seat to the side on a plaid half-couch. They stepped through some bookkeeping necessities on the holly.

"I'm glad to see you're getting out of it," said Jane. "You've done your bit, Lou."

Jane produced clear tumblers and a liter bottle of whiskey, a third full, a blend but of good quality. "You're not adverse to an afternoon drink, are you?"

Jane poured and they clinked glasses. "It's not just the risks," she said. "And the hardships. I think it rips your soul apart. I'm glad you're out in one piece."

Lucius sipped his whiskey.

Two years later the IDA program disbanded. Immigration attempts from the south had gone to a dribble, maybe due to IDA enforcement, maybe because the swamplands had become too noxious to traverse. Problems internalized as the shifting geography forced population adjustments in the north. The government initiated a "citadel" policy, walling up habitable areas and requiring residency or a visa for entry, treating non-authorized entrants as illegals.

Lucius slipped into the citadel bureaucracy, office in Toronto, a co-op in Guelph, half-hour commute by high-speed transport. He started dating a woman three floors below. The relationship lasted eight months. On its last day, Lou said, "Why must it end? I don't rant and break things, do I?"

"Quite the opposite," she said.

One Saturday Lucius dropped down to the garage of the co-op tower, checked out a local transport, and set destination for Maryhill Mall. En route he adjusted his grocery list, transmitted it, leaned back, relaxed, dialed in an adventure movie, IDAs were fighting giant alligators in the abandoned lands. He laughed.

He docked the transport at the mall and was walking to the grocery when a flashback hit.

For Lucius, flashbacks didn't come in dreams. He didn't have nightmares, wake up sweating, falling, like other agents he'd listened to in therapy. He slept well. The flashbacks hit him while he was awake, sometimes sitting around, sometimes walking around, sometimes in public places like now. They popped in, swapped realities, popped out.

The flashback that hit him in the mall was the most recurring, pasty gray hair and beard rising from swamp water, open throat screaming, AK-2047-W flaming. When Ole Ned popped out, Lucius found himself at a standstill, lower lip trembling, heart at the quick-step. He looked left and right. The few odd stares but no loony police.

At the grocery, he logged his transport number, picked out a few more items, marked "no rush," approved the debit. Wandered to the

Auld Tyme Pub, took a booth, ordered a single-malt whiskey, water on the side, plus a pint. Resumed the movie. The IDAs were gaining on the alligators.

A waitress walked by without offering a glance. She was pretty, about his age. Black like him.

Exodus

Their jeans and plaids settled in two plastic chairs, yellow and orange, and they looked around the pod. Not quite a pod, more like two dividers abutting the pale wall, open to the aisle. The words on the wall, *Welcome to Mercy Hospital*, transposed into a woman in business suit, dark hair cut to a pixie, a smile. She said, "Do you speak English?"

Carl ran thick fingers through brown beard into thick hair.

"Yes, ma'am," said Marion. "We sure do."

"Very good," said the woman. "Are you the prospective patient?"

"Yes, ma'am."

"Then I'll ask you to stare straight at me without blinking."

Marion's name, date of birth, and address surfaced under the woman, followed by the last four digits of her social security number.

"Please verify," said the woman.

"That's me for sure."

The woman exhibited a frown. "There seems to be a problem, Marion. We're not showing current financial coverage for you."

"No, ma'am. When my hours got cut, it was too little to stay on their insurance. And my husband—" Marion nodded at Carl.

"Yes," said the woman. "I see Carl has been without coverage for over four years. So—"

"But I went to my internist, and she said I had to get operated on."

Carl leaned into the conversation. "Post haste, she told us. Those were the words she used. The condition—"

"Yes," said the woman. "Quite serious. On behalf of Mercy, I'd like to express our sympathy regarding the diagnosis, and the poor prognosis. However, we cannot proceed without insurance, or surety."

"How much surety?" said Carl.

"For this condition, one hundred eighty-four thousand three hundred thirty-four dollars and fifteen cents. However, I must warn you the final charges will exceed this."

"Ma'am," said Marion. "We don't have that kind of money."

"I'm sorry, then, we cannot proceed," said the woman. "Please let yourselves out the way you came in."

• • • •

TWO DAYS LATER, CARL and Marion motored north in their faded blue Fusion with the auto-driver set for 118 Jewett Avenue in Jersey City. They had a plan. Half-baked but a plan, and the hopeful feeling it engenders at the onset.

Marion stared into the middle distance and Carl said, "What are you reading?"

"*Wuthering Heights*," she said. "And you? Checking the news?"

"Such as it is."

Carl's internal receiver clicked, interrupting the news feed. "Yeah," said Carl.

"Sorry for the intrusion." A pleasant baritone filled Carl's ears. "Am I speaking to Carl Murray?"

"You are."

"And that's you in your vehicle going up ninety-five?"

"It is." Marion looked over and Carl switched to exterior audio. Bureau of Travel Enforcement, he mouthed.

"And who's that with you?" said the baritone.

In years past, under different circumstances, Carl would ask, is there a problem, officer? Is there something wrong with my vehicle? Do you have cause to question me? But today he stayed cool.

"That's my wife with me."

"And you know someone at 118 Jewett?"

"We do. My wife's sister lives there."

"Ah. Isabel, right?"

"Right."

"How long are you staying?"

"A few days. Not sure. Might go over to Manhattan if we can get in."

"You should be able to get a day visa. An overnight might be difficult." The voice rose a pitch as in a personable exchange. "Expensive too."

"I hear you."

"Well, Carl, we apologize for the intrusion, and hope you have a good visit. There's been some problems lately and—Carl, could you do us a favor?"

"What would that be?"

"If you change your plans, give us a heads-up."

The Fusion found a parking spot near Isabel's apartment building. Carl and Marion exited and pulled backpacks from the luggage compartment.

"Nice touch telling them about Manhattan," said Marion.

"I think so," said Carl. "Now they shouldn't be giving us the third degree when we go for the visa."

• • • •

ISABEL HAD AN INCH of height on Marion and a more hawkish face. She opened her arms to her sister. She turned to Carl for a hug. "I wish I could do more," she said.

Carl nodded, looking around the apartment, neat, well attended, what used to be middle class, now high-end country. Carl felt like saying, *maybe you can do more—a couple hundred thou would be nice.* But regretted the thought. No doubt she had savings in six figures, but enough to cover surgery, chemo, radiation? It would drain her. And then what would she do for her own emergency? She might be drawing now from her savings.

Isabel said, "So you're set on this? This course of action?"

"What else?" said Carl.

Marion pulled a chair out from the dining table and sat down. "What else?" she said.

"Are you in pain, dear?"

"Some. I have meds."

"Ask Sam when you see him. He can get anything."

Except a couple hundred thou. Carl said, "You two getting along these days, then?"

"Better now than when we were married. He knows when you're coming?"

"We keep in touch," said Carl. "Make it sound like a vacation visit in case anyone's listening."

Carl looked into the middle distance and found the visa site for Manhattan. He applied for an overnighter. A red triangle flashed.

"They'll only give us the day pass," said Carl.

"That's all we need," said Marion.

Carl blinked for two day passes. To Isabel, he said, "Do you know anything about the Northway tickets? I didn't want to mention it directly in our correspondence."

Isabel shook her head. "Sam was over here last week and said not to worry. That's all I know."

Isabel walked to the living room window and peered into the street. "What did you do with your car?"

"I set it to park itself in that cheap lot south of here. Then Thursday night to take itself back to North Carolina."

Marion's chin lifted like she had just come awake. "What if they see nobody's in it?"

"It'll be dark. And they won't be checking us going back. And even if they do, it'll be too late."

Isabel trekked to the kitchen and returned with cups of tea. A second trip brought out cookies. Marion said, "I guess I'll take a med."

She popped the lid from a small container and slipped a white tablet onto her tongue.

"How does Sam do it?" said Carl. "Stay in the city?"

"It's a little convoluted," said Isabel. "Sam can explain it when you see him."

"He still playing that bass guitar?"

"Oh yeah. But most of his work comes from waiting tables and bouncing."

"You mean like a bouncer?" said Marion.

"A bit small for that," said Carl.

"You don't need to be big," said Isabel. "He has this prong thing called a TestiTaser that works like a charm. And the crowds in New York these days, well they're not a rowdy bunch."

"I'm guessing not," said Carl.

"Oh you get some occasional riffraff in on a pass. But the regulars, they all have incomes upside of a million. Intoxication is the only real problem." Isabel took her sister's hand. "Have you thought this through?"

"Through and through," said Marion. "I've got to rest a bit."

Isabel returned from helping Marion to the bedroom and said, "Things are changing in Canada."

"I been hearing," said Carl.

"The government's setting new rules. They're putting up a fence. There's vigilantes."

Isabel turned on the Holovision and locked onto a man-in-the-street interview in Montreal, a thin man of about forty, proper, in a suit.

"His face," said Isabel. "He looks like a mad dog."

"They take our jobs," the man said through wet lips. "They rape our women."

The interviewer said, "Now, sir—"

"They don't even speak proper English."

"But sir," said the interviewer, "these people are destitute. They have nowhere—"

"They should've thought of that before, shouldn't they've? Shouldn't they've? It's not our concern."

On and on. Carl said, "They don't seem as civil as they used to."

"How can you hope to even get in?"

"Sam has a contact in the north country."

"That would be Bernard," said Isabel.

"You know him?" Carl caught Isabel's glance. "You don't like him?"

"Oh, he's fine. He's more than fine. But I don't see what he can do."

• • • •

SAM WORE A RED POLY shirt, blue pants, black hair, and an iridescent smile. Ever the dresser, always the smile, no matter the circumstances. He'd met them at Penn Station. "I've got you booked on the four oh nine to Plattsburgh," he said.

"And we'll get to Plattsburgh afore they realize we're off our visa?" said Carl.

"Better," said Sam. He brought Carl and Marion into a huddle. "I know a systems guy in transport. When you're scanned on the Northway, it'll show the four oh nine for Plattsburgh, but when the scan goes to central, it'll show the five thirteen back to Jersey City."

They had exited Penn Station on Eighth Avenue. "We've got a few hours," said Sam. "Do you feel up to seeing anything?"

Carl was about to suggest finding a place to rest, but Marion said, "I'd sure like to see that sea wall that's supposed to be the newest wonder of the world?"

Sam said, "Okay, we can walk right over to the High Line. You'll get a good view of the west wall from there. Or take a cab."

"I can still walk a few blocks."

Marion proceeded at a slow but happy pace. At the High Line, she insisted on taking the stairs, one trudge at a time, resting every third step. The trio walked toward the river and looked over what used to be the West Side Highway. Its former tarmac formed the base of an inclined dike forty feet high, narrowing to ten feet and a monorail at top. Carl had read that the monorail transported a quick-reaction roboforce in case anyone got through the cameras, heat sensors, and body zappers.

"Well," said Marion, "this is something, seeing it in person."

"Nice and dry this side," said Carl. "What's it like yonder?"

"The river's up the dike about eight feet at high tide."

"I guess she'll hold for a while."

"I guess she will," said Sam.

"And the whole island's like this?" said Marion.

"Up to the highlands," said Sam.

Carl looked uptown and down. Newer skyscrapers everywhere. Skyways and skyports everywhere.

"How do you afford it, Sam?" said Carl. "If you don't mind my asking."

"It's a little tricky," said Carl. "Right now we have twelve bodies sharing a one-bedroom."

"Jesus," said Marion.

"It's not that bad. We're working all the time, all hours. When you come in, you just inflate a mattress and grab a spot."

"Don't the city or association or whatever object to all them people in one apartment?" said Carl.

"That's the tricky part," said Sam. "You get your residency permit elsewhere. It's another market."

Carl shook his head.

Sam said, "You find somebody who has an apartment but wants to live alone but needs some extra money."

"And?"

"And you pay them. They list you as a resident but you never go there."

"How much is that?"

"Two a month. And four a month for the place you're actually staying in."

Marion drifted to a bench and sat down. A breeze off the Hudson ruffled her hair.

Sam lowered his voice. "It bothers me that I can't help you more."

"You're helping all you can."

"I can get an internist, but I can't get the big stuff on trade."

"You done all you can." They stood silent a minute. "What about our contact up north? Bernard is it?"

Sam said, "You'll like him. Look for an old pickup, a Tacoma, one you have drive yourself. Look for a skinny guy a little older than us. T-shirt probably, baseball cap."

• • • •

THE TACOMA HAD AN EXTENDED cab with jump seats behind the front seats. Carl helped Marion into the passenger seat and clambered behind her. Bernard started the gasoline motor and moved the truck onto an old state highway of buckled tar.

"You like doing your own driving," said Carl.

"I don't want any connections," said Bernard, pointing skyward, "in or out."

"They can still track you with cameras and radar."

"Not if they're shot out," said Bernard. "By the way, you got your signals shut off?"

"My privacy settings don't allow tracking."

"Not good enough. Turn 'em off."

Bernard crossed to the opposing lane to avoid a large buckle in the road. He crossed back.

"The news is not good," he said. "Things have been changing."

"We been hearing that," said Carl.

"Up to a few months ago," said Bernard, "I could set you this side of the border. You could walk across and a samaritan on the other side would take you in. Just a matter of logistics."

"And the samaritans, they're gone?"

"The first problem," said Bernard. "The land border's been defoliated and mined."

"Mined?" said Marion.

"Set off by motion detection. Next, it used to be you could get into their health system if you had a sponsor, or just walked into a hospital. Now you get deported. Third—"

Was there need for a third?

"The mood's changed. It's dangerous to be a samaritan or sponsor."

"Then what are we doing?" said Carl.

The truck sidled onto a side road and stopped. Bernard pushed open his door and slipped to the ground. Carl heard a grinding noise as Bernard pulled at a metal object from under the front seat. A rifle with a scope emerged.

"I'll be right back." Carl walked fifty feet along the road then dropped into the woods.

Marion turned a quarter in her seat. "I'm getting to be too much a drag on everyone. Especially you."

Carl took her hand. "Don't want to hear that."

A few hundred feet ahead, the rifle popped.

"I'm just saying," said Marion. "Nobody lives forever."

The rifle popped twice more.

"Don't want to hear it."

Bernard reappeared. He stowed the rifle and started the truck.

"I'm taking you to our so-called underground clinic," he said. "Doctor Rodriguez."

"What can they do for me?" said Marion.

"I don't know but I wanted to try that first."

• • • •

THE CLINIC LOOKED LIKE an old middle school with a flat, open design. Marion and Carl waited in one of the former classrooms along with fifty other patients, separated from the others by a hospital curtain. Carl sat on a plastic chair while Marion leaned back at forty-five degrees on a gurney. She dozed. Three hours after arriving, Doctor Rodriguez dropped behind the curtain with a technician.

"Sorry for the wait," she said. "Take that gown off, Marion."

The technician ran a wand over Marion's body while Rodriguez looked in the middle distance. The doctor glanced over and the technician left.

As Marion dressed, Rodriguez sat on the edge of the gurney. "We can give you some heavy duty medication for the pain."

"Is that it?"

Rodriguez stood and hooked a finger. "Carl, you want to come with me." Carl followed the doctor to an alcove where she unlocked an overhead cabinet and removed two vials of tablets.

Rodriguez said, "We send the occasional cancer patient down to Cornell but our resources only allow one in eighty. How do you triage that?"

Carl nodded.

"If you could leave a donation up front, whatever you can."

"Sure enough."

"Listen to me, Carl. I'm giving you two hundred tablets. One every six hours as needed." She paused. "If you take more than that, they're lethal. Three will probably kill you. Five for sure. Do you understand what I'm saying?"

"Three probably, five for sure," said Carl.

Rodriguez put a hand on Carl's arm, dropped it, and disappeared.

• • • •

CARL HAD IMAGINED BERNARD a recluse in a storage container at the edge of civilization, but he lived in a normal-looking townhouse with a normal-looking wife and a half normal-looking grown-up son. Carl scraped his kitchen chair alongside Bernard's. An overhead light illuminated a large-scale paper map open on the kitchen table. Across the breakfast counter, the darkened living room flickered from an ancient flat-screen monitor. Bernard's son and wife sat on a couch watching it. Marion lay asleep in a recliner. Carl started to get up as she wriggled and moaned, but she fell back into her sleep, and Carl turned his attention to the map.

"Here we are," said Bernard, placing a forefinger. He dragged it westward. "And here the border runs into the river." Bernard looked up. "But the north shore is mined and guarded these days."

Bernard's finger pushed down and to the left—upriver—into Lake Erie. "Best bet is the lake. Come ashore north side, here, just past this jutting-out part."

"How do we do that?"

"You'll be getting a skiff with a small motor. You'll be starting at this point on the east shore."

Carl sat up. He was no sailor, and this looked like a large body of water. Bernard didn't seem to appreciate his concern. "You can't turn on a GPS," he said. "But dead reckoning won't be hard."

Carl leaned over the map again. Bernard said, "All you have to do is keep a heading of due east for eight hours at three-quarter speed." He looked up. Carl nodded, knowing that much. "Then change your heading to due north. Look for a tall building with a soft blue light atop. You might not be able to make out the building, but you'll see the light."

"What about mines and guards?"

"It's a populated area with docks and waterfront properties and whatnot. Just put in wherever it looks safe."

"Safe?"

"Another reason to send you west into Ontario is I don't think the panic's taken hold there yet. You're more likely to get a friendly reception."

Carl leaned back in the kitchen chair. What had seemed hopeful at the onset had dimmed as distance diminished.

Bernard placed a beat-up rectangle of red-framed plastic on the table. "Do you know how to read a magnetic compass? The declination is eleven degrees west."

Carl nodded.

"That means you have to set it so three-fifty is north."

Carl nodded.

"No signals in or out. Internal or otherwise."

Carl nodded a third time.

"You can hole up here," said Bernard, "until we get a good night."

"Dark?"

"Still," said Bernard. "We want the water to be perfectly still, or you'll get lost or worse."

In the living room, Marion's eyelashes flickered in synchronicity with the flat-screen. She moaned. Carl reached in his jeans for the medication.

• • • •

CARL LAY ON HIS STOMACH on the dock and placed a foot-long boat on the surface of Lake Erie—not much more than a hull and a motor. Alongside him, Bernard reached down and touched a switch. The boat accelerated toward the gathering sunset, trailing by ten-minute intervals two mates. Bernard stood and Carl followed his lead.

"Okay," said Bernard, "let's bring down your transport."

Carl tossed his head toward the lake. "Do those dummy boats do any good?"

"Their coast guard gets tired of checking every blob."

Bernard and Carl walked inland twenty feet to a run-down cottage and grabbed a rope snaking out from its under-storage. As they heaved, Carl looked into the passenger seat of Bernard's pickup at Marion slumped with her eyes closed. The boat they dragged was a fourteen-foot fiberglass skiff with a small inboard motor and extra batteries. They lowered it from the dock and Bernard looped the rope over the tie-off pile. A trip to the truck brought down backpacks, water, and sandwiches.

"You got your compass?" said Bernard.

Carl lifted it from his shirt pocket.

"Keep that string around your neck. Now if you have to abort," said Bernard, "for any reason." He looked west across the lake and swept his left arm, "Head due south until you hit land. Let me show you something else." Bernard leaned into the boat and opened the motor housing. "See that switch. That's the scuttle switch. Get out of the boat, give her a heading, and throw that switch."

"And?"

"And twenty minutes later she'll take herself to the bottom."

Carl tried to form a question regarding the circumstances of scuttling. But maybe he knew enough. He walked to the truck and opened the passenger door. Marion opened her eyes.

"I hate to be a baby," she said, "but I'm needing more of those meds."

Carl pulled the vial from his jeans and tipped two tablets into his left hand. Marion took them followed by gulps of bottled water. She swung her body and dropped her feet. Bernard had come up and the two men supported her as she swayed to the dock.

• • • •

IN THE WEE HOURS, THE blue light on the north shore appeared like a low-lying star. Another hour, Carl figured, and he'd change their heading from west to north. Marion snoozed.

A ripple floated across the surface of the lake and lapped the boat. Carl cut the motor. He prayed for Marion to remain asleep.

The tick-tock of a diesel motor ran north of and parallel to their boat. The sound changed in pitch and grew louder. Soon the skiff bobbed on waves emanating from a larger boat. The diesel motor dropped to half throttle, then quarter, then idle, and the hull of a sixty-foot vessel emerged from the cast of night. A soft white light poked along the top of the water and landed on Carl and Marion.

A stiff voice hailed them. "Ahoy."

"Ahoy yourself," said Carl.

"Canadian Coast Guard. Are you adrift?"

Carl gave no answer.

"Do you have power?"

What to say?

"Look," said the Canadian, "you've got to turn south. It would be better to do it under your own power."

"My wife's sick. Real sick."

Carl thought he could make out a railing and a figure, but for the most part, the voice hovered. "Quite sorry to hear that," it said. "But you can't proceed."

The boat shifted to port as Marion's body twisted from back to side. She lifted her head.

Above the superstructure of the coast guard vessel, the blue light continued its faint glow. Carl raised his eyes and located the little dipper, and on its tail the north star.

"I say, do you have power?"

"Yes," said Carl, "I have power."

Carl switched on the motor and twisted the rudder. He put the north star behind and checked the compass hanging from his neck.

"Carl, honey," said Marion, "the pain is awful."

Carl reached in his pocket.

Cover and Publication Credits

Cover design by Alejandra Mandelblum.

"Azaleas" was first published in *Korea Lit*, April 1, 2016 and reprinted in *Front Porch Review*, Vol. 10 October 2018.

"A Joke for Chong" was first published in *The Icarus Anthology*, Issue 2, August 2017.

"Class of '65" was first published in *And Then*, Volume 19, 2017.

"Men at War" was first published in *As You Were: The Military Review*, Vol. 6 Spring 2017.

"Low Speed Jet" was first published in *New Zenith Magazine*, Volume 1, Summer 2016 and reprinted in the 2019 issue of *So It Goes: The Literary Journal of the Kurt Vonnegut Museum and Library*.

"Government Issue" was first published in *Podium Literary Journal*, Issue 15.

"Rearguard" was first published in *The Fictional Café*, October 8, 2018.

"Wasteland" was first published in *Adelaide Literary Award Anthology 2019*, SHORT STORIES, Volume One and *Adelaide Literary Magazine* No. 34, March 2020.

"What About India?" was first published in *The Manchester Review*, Issue 16, June 2016.

"There You Go" was first published in *TIMBER A Journal of New Writing*, 9.2 Summer 2019.

"Hippasus of Metapontum" was first published in *Lowestoft Chronicle*, June 2019, Issue 38.

"Negative Entropy" was first published in *The Wayward Sword*, Vol 2 Issue 1, Writing Knights, Grand Showcase 2018. Reprinted in *Twist in Time*, Issue 5, September 1, 2019.

"Mind Over Matter" was first published in *Prick of the Spindle*, Issue 8, Print Edition, Spring/Summer 2015.

"The Pugilist" was first published in *The Bombay Review* Issue 34 (September, 2020).

"Sunrise Cliff" was first published in *The Wild Word*, February, 2024.

"Ole Ned" was first published in *Pif Magazine*, Issue No. 230, July 1, 2016.

"Exodus" was first published in *Sweet Tree Review*, Volume 2 Issue 3, Summer 2017.

About the Author

Robert Perron is the author of the novel *The Blue House Raid*. His short stories have appeared in numerous literary journals. His past life includes military service, a career in high tech, marriages, and children. Today he bounces between New Hampshire and New York City, where he stays with his longtime girlfriend.

Read more at https://robertperron.com.

Milton Keynes UK
Ingram Content Group UK Ltd.
UKHW022018071224
452128UK00001B/49